DEAD ENCOUNTER VOLUME 2

This is a work of fiction. Similarities to real people, places, or events are entirely coincidental.

DEAD ENCOUNTER

First edition. November 17, 2024.

Copyright © 2024 JT WULF.

ISBN: 979-8230569299

Written by JT WULF.

REFLECTION OF THE SOUL

The flames danced before us, casting ghastly shadows across familiar faces now twisted into masks of anticipation. I could feel their eyes boring into me, waiting, hungry. The weight of expectation pressed down, squeezing the air from my lungs.

"I'll go first," I heard myself say, my voice barely a whisper.

As the words left my lips, I caught Brianna's gaze across the fire. Her hazel eyes flickered with something - was it fear? Or recognition? I quickly looked away, unable to bear the intensity of that stare.

I took a shaky breath, steeling myself. "There was a girl I knew, years ago. We were... close." My eyes darted to Brianna again, unbidden. "Too close, maybe."

The crackle of the fire filled the silence as I paused, gathering my thoughts. How much should I reveal? How much did they already suspect?

"She became... obsessed," I continued, my voice low. "At first it was flattering. Notes in my locker, surprise visits. But then..."

I trailed off, lost in memories. The incessant texts. The gifts left on my doorstep. The figure I glimpsed outside my window late at night.

"Then what, Ella?" someone prodded. I started, having momentarily forgotten my audience.

"Then it got scary," I said simply. "She wouldn't leave me alone. Everywhere I went, she was there. Watching. Waiting."

A chill wind rustled through the trees, and we all instinctively huddled closer to the fire. I noticed Brianna had wrapped her arms tightly around herself, her face pale in the flickering light.

"What happened to her?" another voice asked.

I swallowed hard. "I don't know," I lied. "She just… disappeared one day."

But I did know. I would never forget that night, the desperation in her eyes, the things we both said and did. Some sins can never be washed clean.

As I finished my tale, an uneasy silence fell over the group. I could see the questions in their eyes, the growing realization that this was more than just a spooky story.

"Jesus, Ella," someone finally muttered. "That's heavy."

I forced a wan smile. "Yeah, well. You wanted scary stories, right?"

But as I met Brianna's gaze once more across the flames, I knew the real horror was just beginning.

Marcus cleared his throat, drawing our attention. His eyes darted nervously to the shadowy treeline before settling back on the fire.

"I guess it's my turn," he said, his voice tight. "I... I've never told anyone this before."

I watched as he took a deep breath, his shoulders tensing. The firelight cast eerie shadows across his face, making him look older, haunted.

"When I was ten, I used to play in these woods," Marcus began, his words measured. "One day, I felt... watched. Like eyes were boring into the back of my skull."

A twig snapped in the darkness beyond our circle. Marcus flinched, his gaze shooting to the trees. We all held our breath, but nothing emerged.

"It followed me," he continued, lower now. "For weeks. Always just out of sight. A dark figure, tall and thin. I'd catch glimpses, you know? Between the trees, or reflected in my bedroom window at night."

My skin prickled. I could almost feel it now - that sensation of being hunted.

"Did you ever see its face?" I asked, transfixed.

Marcus shook his head. "No. But sometimes... sometimes I swear I can still hear it breathing."

As if on cue, a gust of wind whispered through the leaves. Marcus tensed, his eyes wild as they scanned the forest.

"It's just the wind," Jonah murmured, but he didn't sound convinced.

I found myself leaning forward. "What happened? How did it end?"

Marcus met my gaze, and the raw fear I saw there made my blood run cold.

"Who says it ever did?"

The crackling fire couldn't chase away the chill that had settled in my bones. Brianna cleared her throat, drawing our attention. Her face was a mask of calm, but I noticed her hands trembling as she tucked a wayward strand of red hair behind her ear.

"My turn, I suppose," she said, her voice steady despite the tension in her shoulders. "It started with scratching sounds. Just little noises at first, easy to dismiss."

I watched her closely, sensing the weight of unspoken trauma in every carefully chosen word.

"But it grew," Brianna continued, her hazel eyes reflecting the dancing flames. "Thumps and creaks that echoed through the floorboards. Always from below. Always at night."

"What was it?" Marcus whispered, his earlier fear momentarily forgotten.

Brianna's lips tightened. "Something... hungry. Something that wanted in."

I felt a shudder run through me, imagining the terror of feeling unsafe in your own home.

"Did you ever see it?" I asked, dreading the answer.

"Once," Brianna said, her voice dropping. "Just a glimpse. Eyes gleaming in the dark, claws scraping wood. But that was enough."

She fell silent, lost in memory. I wanted to reach out, to offer comfort, but the space between us felt insurmountable.

"What did you do?" Jonah prodded gently.

Brianna's gaze snapped back to the present, a flicker of steel behind her eyes. "I survived," she said simply. "I learned to be stronger than my fear."

The silence that followed was heavy with unspoken understanding. Then, almost imperceptibly, Sasha shifted. All eyes turned to her, expectant.

Her violet eyes met each of ours in turn, lingering a heartbeat too long. When she finally spoke, her soft voice carried an otherworldly chill.

"You know me," Sasha whispered.

Those three words hung in the air, laden with meaning I couldn't quite grasp. I glanced at the others, saw the same dawning horror reflected in their faces.

What did she mean? What did we know?

The night seemed to press in closer, the shadows deepening at the edges of our circle. And in that moment, I realized with sickening clarity that our ghost stories were far from over.

A whisper drifted through the trees, so faint I almost convinced myself I'd imagined it. But then I saw Marcus stiffen, his eyes darting to the darkness beyond our campfire.

"Did you hear that?" he hissed, voice tight with barely concealed panic.

I strained my ears, heart hammering. There it was again - a sibilant murmur, wordless yet somehow familiar.

"It's just the wind," Ella said, but her trembling voice betrayed her doubt.

Another whisper, closer this time. I could almost make out words, fragments of secrets I'd buried deep.

"We should go," Brianna urged, already half-rising. "This isn't—"

Her words cut off as a chorus of hushed voices swelled around us, a cacophony of whispers that seemed to come from everywhere and nowhere.

"It's not real," I muttered, more to myself than the others. "It can't be real."

But as we huddled closer to the dying fire, I felt the weight of unseen eyes upon us. The voices grew, a susurrus of half-heard confessions and long-forgotten sins.

"What's happening?" Jonah whimpered, his earlier bravado evaporating.

I opened my mouth to reassure him, to offer some rational explanation, but the words died on my tongue as flickering lights appeared at the edge of our camp. They danced between the trees, casting grotesque shadows that seemed to reach for us with grasping fingers.

Our phones buzzed in unison, a jarring electronic chorus. With trembling hands, I pulled mine out, dreading what I'd find.

The message glowed on the screen, a truth I'd never spoken aloud: "You let her die. You could have saved her, but you didn't."

Ella's choked sob told me she'd received something equally devastating. Marcus stared at his phone in wide-eyed horror, while Brianna hurled hers away as if it had burned her.

"How?" I croaked. "How could they know?"

The whispering intensified, a sinister lullaby that promised to drag us into the depths of our own guilt. And as the shadows crept closer, I realized with dawning terror that our darkest secrets were no longer our own.

A strangled gasp escaped my lips as I saw her—the obsessive friend I'd tried so hard to forget, watching me from the treeline. Her eyes glowed with an unnatural light, a twisted smile playing on her lips.

"No," I whispered, my voice barely audible. "You're not real. You can't be here."

Marcus's voice cut through my panic. "Oh God, it's him. He's back." His eyes darted wildly, fixed on a point just beyond the flickering firelight. I saw nothing, but the terror in his face was all too real.

Jonah's phone rang, shattering the eerie silence. His face drained of color as he stared at the screen. "It's... it's my father," he choked out.

Brianna's scream pierced the night as her phone lit up with a barrage of threatening messages. "Make it stop," she pleaded, her hands shaking uncontrollably.

I wanted to comfort them, to tell them it wasn't real, but the words wouldn't come. How could I, when my own nightmare stood before me, as real as the trees around us?

Suddenly, Sasha crumpled to the ground, clutching her chest. We rushed to her side, our own terrors momentarily forgotten.

"Sasha!" I cried, reaching for her. But as I touched her shoulder, her head snapped up, and I recoiled in horror.

Her eyes, once a striking violet, now glowed with an otherworldly light. When she spoke, it wasn't Sasha's voice that emerged, but something ancient and terrible.

"Your fears have summoned us," the thing wearing Sasha's face intoned. "Your guilt has given us form. We will claim you all, one by one, until nothing remains but the hollow shells of your former selves."

I stumbled backward, my heart pounding so hard I thought it might burst. This couldn't be happening. It had to be a dream, a hallucination. But as I looked into the terrified faces of my friends, I knew the nightmare had only just begun.

The air grew thick with dread as the entity's words hung over us. My friends' faces contorted in agony, their bodies twisting unnaturally. Ella's skin stretched taut over her bones, her fingers elongating into claws as she scratched at invisible tormentors. Marcus thrashed on the ground, his eyes rolling back in his head as he mumbled incoherently about dark figures in the woods.

"No, please, I'll be good," Brianna whimpered, curling into a fetal position. "Don't hurt me again."

I felt it too—a creeping coldness seeping into my veins, threatening to consume me. My father's voice echoed in my head, a litany of disappointments and shortcomings.

"You'll never measure up, Jonah," it hissed. "You're a stain on our family name."

I clutched my head, willing the voice to stop. "It's not real," I muttered, trying to convince myself. "It's not—"

But it was real. The pain, the fear, the crushing weight of expectations—they were all real, and they were destroying us.

Through the haze of torment, a small voice inside me whispered: "The truth will set you free."

I took a shuddering breath, steeling myself. "No," I said, my voice trembling but growing stronger. "You're wrong, Dad. I am enough."

The darkness recoiled, just slightly. I pressed on, my words becoming a lifeline in the chaos.

"Our family isn't perfect. We're broken, flawed, and that's okay. I won't hide it anymore. I won't be silent."

With each truth I spoke, I felt lighter. The oppressive force weakened, and I saw a glimmer of hope in my friends' eyes. "We all have demons," I declared, my voice ringing out clear and strong. "But they don't define us. We define ourselves."

As the last word left my lips, the malevolent presence shrieked and dissipated, leaving us shaken but free. In that moment of clarity, I realized that sometimes, the greatest horror isn't what lurks in the shadows, but what we hide within ourselves.

The air crackled with tension as Brianna's eyes locked onto something unseen. Her fingers trembled, clutching a tattered photograph. "No," she whispered, her voice barely audible. "You don't control me anymore."

I watched, transfixed, as she stood, her legs unsteady but her gaze unwavering. The photo burst into flames, consuming the image of a man with cold, dead eyes.

"I am not your victim," Brianna declared, her voice gaining strength. "I am a survivor."

The fire in her palm grew, casting eerie shadows across her face. For a moment, I thought I saw a flicker of something dark and monstrous behind her, but it recoiled from the light.

"You can't hurt me now," she continued, her words a litany of defiance. "I choose to live. I choose to be free."

As the last embers of the photograph died, a weight seemed to lift from Brianna's shoulders. She exhaled, a small smile playing at the corners of her lips.

My relief was short-lived. A chill ran down my spine as I felt unseen eyes boring into me. The forest seemed to close in, branches reaching out like gnarled fingers.

"Marcus," a voice whispered, achingly familiar. "Why did you leave me?"

I squeezed my eyes shut, willing the apparition away. But the guilt, the shame—they clung to me like a second skin.

"It wasn't your fault," Brianna's voice cut through the fog. "You were just a child."

I opened my eyes, meeting her steady gaze. "But I ran," I confessed, the words tearing from my throat. "I left him there, alone in the dark."

The shadows twisted, taking the form of a small boy. My younger self, lost and afraid.

"I'm sorry," I whispered, tears streaming down my face. "I'm so sorry I couldn't save you."

As I spoke the words I'd held back for so long, the apparition began to fade. The forest stilled, and I felt a strange sense of peace settle over me.

"We can't change the past," I said softly, "but we can choose how it shapes us."

The weight of years of guilt lifted, leaving me breathless but free. In the darkness of that cursed forest, we had faced our demons and emerged, battered but unbroken.

I turned to Ella, her green eyes shimmering with unshed tears in the dying firelight. The tension between us hung thick in the air, heavier than the oppressive darkness surrounding our small circle.

"Ella," I whispered, my voice hoarse from screaming. "I'm sorry. For everything."

She stared at me, her face a mask of pain and confusion. "Brianna, I—"

"No," I interrupted, reaching out to grasp her trembling hand. "I pushed you away. I was so afraid of being hurt again that I hurt you instead."

Ella's fingers tightened around mine. "I should have seen what you were going through," she murmured. "Some friend I was."

A bitter laugh escaped my lips. "We were both blind, weren't we?"

As we clung to each other, I felt something shift in the air. The malevolent presence that had been suffocating us seemed to recoil, hissing in frustration.

"It's weakening," Marcus whispered urgently. "Quick, we need to help Sasha!"

We turned as one to face our friend. Sasha's body was contorted, her eyes rolled back in her head as inky tendrils of darkness writhed around her.

"Together," I said, gripping Ella's hand tighter. "We fight together."

We formed a circle around Sasha, our hands linked. The entity lashed out, its icy talons raking across my mind. I gasped, nearly losing my grip on consciousness.

"Hold on," Ella's voice anchored me. "We're stronger than it is."

As dawn's first light crept through the trees, we poured every ounce of our strength, our love, our newly forged bonds into Sasha. The darkness screamed, a sound of pure malevolence that made my ears bleed.

Then, silence.

Sasha's eyes fluttered open, confusion and fear giving way to recognition. "You saved me," she whispered, her voice raw.

As we collapsed around her, exhausted but triumphant, I knew we'd all been irrevocably changed. The horrors we'd faced had forged us anew, stronger in our broken places.

The sun rose on a world that seemed both familiar and utterly strange. We were free, but the shadows of the night would linger in our souls forever.

NIGHT AT THE ELDRIDGE

The rusted iron gates of the Eldridge Historical Museum loomed before them, a dark silhouette against the starless night sky. Jake's heart thundered in his chest as he gripped the cold metal bars, his palms slick with sweat.

"We're really doing this," he whispered, a mix of exhilaration and trepidation coursing through him.

Amir adjusted his glasses, peering through the bars. "According to my research, the security system hasn't been updated since 1985. We should be able to bypass it easily."

Shane laid a reassuring hand on Jake's shoulder. "We've got this, mate. Just like we planned."

Jake nodded, drawing strength from his friends' presence. With practiced ease, he maneuvered the wire through the ancient lock, feeling for the telltale click. The gate creaked open, the sound unnaturally loud in the stillness.

They slipped inside, hugging the shadows cast by towering oaks. Jake's senses were on high alert, every rustle of leaves and distant car horn amplified in the darkness. The museum's imposing facade loomed ahead, its windows like hollow eyes watching their approach.

"Remember," Jake whispered as they reached the side entrance, "we're in and out. No lingering."

Amir's nimble fingers made quick work of the lock. As the door swung open, Jake hesitated, suddenly overwhelmed by the weight of what they were about to do. But the thrill of adventure beckoned, impossible to resist.

They stepped into the museum's hushed interior, enveloped by the musty scent of aged artifacts and polished wood. Their flashlights cut through the gloom, revealing display cases filled with relics from bygone eras. Jake's beam swept across a collection of ancient weaponry, the blades gleaming dully.

"Creepy," Shane muttered, his usual bravado tinged with unease.

Jake forced a chuckle. "What, scared of a few dusty old relics?"

But as they ventured deeper into the museum's labyrinthine corridors, an oppressive silence settled over them. Their footsteps echoed off marble floors, each sound seeming to reverberate endlessly. Jake couldn't shake the feeling that unseen eyes were watching, tracking their every move.

Amir's voice cut through the quiet. "Did you know this building was once a sanatorium? They say the ghosts of patients still haunt these halls."

"Real comforting, Amir," Shane retorted, but his attempt at levity fell flat.

Jake's mind raced, imagining spectral figures lurking just beyond the reach of their flashlights. He shook his head, trying to dispel the unsettling thoughts. "Come on, guys. Let's find what we came for and get out of here."

But as they rounded a corner, Jake froze. For a split second, he could have sworn he saw a figure dart across the far end of the corridor. He blinked, and it was gone.

"Did you see that?" he whispered, his voice barely audible.

Amir and Shane exchanged worried glances. "See what?" Amir asked.

Jake swallowed hard. "Nothing. Just my imagination."

But as they pressed on, the prickling sensation at the back of his neck intensified. Something was wrong. Very wrong. And Jake couldn't shake the feeling that they had just made a terrible mistake.

The ornate grandfather clock in the main hall chimed midnight, its sonorous tones echoing through the cavernous museum. Jake's heart skipped a beat as an unnatural hush fell over the building, smothering even the sound of their breathing.

"Did it just get... quieter?" Shane whispered, his voice unnaturally loud in the stillness.

Jake nodded, unable to shake the feeling of dread creeping up his spine. "Yeah, it's like the whole place is holding its breath."

Amir's eyes darted nervously behind his glasses. "Guys, look at the lights."

The antique sconces lining the walls flickered erratically, casting dancing shadows that seemed to move with a life of their own. Jake's palms grew clammy as he gripped his flashlight tighter.

"Maybe we should head back," he suggested, trying to keep the tremor out of his voice.

But before anyone could respond, a low whisper drifted through the air, seemingly from everywhere and nowhere at once. Jake's blood ran cold as he strained to make out the words.

"What was that?" Shane asked, his freckled face pale in the wavering light.

Jake opened his mouth to reply, but the words died in his throat as he caught sight of movement in his peripheral vision. Slowly, he turned towards the World War I exhibit.

"Oh my God," Amir breathed.

The life-sized diorama of trench warfare was no longer static. Soldiers, their uniforms caked with mud and blood, marched silently through No Man's Land. The eerie tableau moved with fluid grace, weapons at the ready, eyes fixed on some unseen enemy.

Jake felt his legs go weak. "This... this isn't possible."

Shane grabbed his arm, fingers digging in painfully. "Jake, look!"

In the adjacent hall, suits of medieval armor creaked to life, brandishing swords and maces as they stepped from their pedestals.

The clanking of metal mingled with the whispered voices, creating a cacophony of otherworldly sound.

"We need to get out of here," Jake managed, his voice barely above a whisper. But as he turned to flee, he realized with horror that the exhibits behind them had come alive as well, cutting off their escape.

They were trapped, surrounded by history come to terrifying life.

Jake's heart hammered against his ribs as he surveyed the nightmarish scene unfolding around them. The weight of responsibility pressed down on him, threatening to crush his resolve. But as he looked at Amir and Shane's terrified faces, a fierce protectiveness surged through him.

"Stay close," Jake commanded, his voice steadier than he felt. He reached out, grasping his friends' shoulders. "We're getting out of here together, no matter what."

Amir's eyes darted around frantically. "But how? We're surrounded!"

Jake took a deep breath, pushing down his own fear. "We'll find a way. Remember the emergency exit we passed earlier? If we can reach it..."

A thunderous crash interrupted him as a nearby suit of armor toppled to the ground. Shane flinched, pressing closer to Jake.

"It's okay," Jake assured him, even as doubt gnawed at his insides. "Just follow my lead."

They inched forward, Jake positioning himself slightly ahead of the others. The animated exhibits seemed to watch their every move, but made no attempt to stop them. Yet.

"This doesn't make sense," Amir muttered, his brow furrowed in concentration. "Wait... Jake, look at the displays. Do you notice anything?"

Jake glanced around, confused. "What do you mean?"

Amir's voice took on an excited edge, despite the circumstances. "The exhibits, they're not random. There's a pattern to how they're moving."

"Is now really the time for-" Shane began, but Amir cut him off.

"No, listen! The World War I soldiers, they're marching west. And the medieval knights are heading east. It's like... like they're reenacting their battles."

Jake felt a glimmer of hope. "So if we can predict their movements..."

"We might be able to find a safe path through," Amir finished, his eyes gleaming with the thrill of solving a puzzle.

Jake squeezed Amir's shoulder. "Good work. Keep observing. Any information could be the key to getting us out alive."

As they cautiously navigated the labyrinth of living history, Jake's mind raced. How were they going to explain this to anyone? Would anyone even believe them? And more pressingly, how long could he keep his friends safe in this impossible situation?

"Jake," Shane whispered urgently, "I think I see a clear path to the next room."

Jake nodded, steeling himself. "Alright, on my count. One... two..."

Shane's steady hand gripped Jake's shoulder, his touch a comforting anchor amidst the swirling chaos. "We've got this," he murmured, his voice a soothing balm that seemed to push back the encroaching darkness. "Remember when we thought that summer camp obstacle course was scary? This is just... a more intense version of that."

Jake couldn't help but let out a nervous chuckle, feeling some of the tension ease from his body. "Yeah, just with more undead soldiers and less mosquito bites."

Amir's eyes darted nervously between his friends and the shifting exhibits. "I'm not sure I'd prefer the mosquitoes right now."

"Hey," Shane said softly, his freckled face etched with determination. "We're in this together. No matter what happens, we've got each other's backs. Right?"

The unwavering loyalty in Shane's eyes made Jake's throat tighten. "Right," he managed to croak out.

As they crept deeper into the museum's depths, the air grew heavy with an oppressive stillness. The boys' footsteps echoed unnaturally loud against the marble floors, each step feeling like a thunderclap in the eerie silence.

Suddenly, a figure materialized before them, causing all three to stumble back in shock. An elderly woman with flowing silver hair stood blocking their path, her piercing blue eyes seeming to look right through them.

"Mrs. Eldridge?" Jake gasped, recognizing the museum's enigmatic curator.

Her lips curved into a smile that didn't quite reach her eyes. "Welcome, young explorers. Have you come seeking knowledge... or something more?"

Shane stepped forward protectively. "We're just trying to find our way out, ma'am."

Mrs. Eldridge's gaze swept over them, lingering uncomfortably long on each boy. "But are you truly lost? Or perhaps... exactly where you're meant to be?"

Jake felt a chill run down his spine. "What do you mean?"

"The past echoes in the present," she intoned, her voice taking on an otherworldly quality. "Shadows of what was become whispers of what may be. The key lies in the hands of those who dare to listen."

Amir leaned in close to Jake, whispering, "Is it just me, or is she making even less sense than usual?"

Jake shook his head slightly, trying to decipher the cryptic words. "Mrs. Eldridge, please. We need help. The exhibits... they're alive somehow."

A knowing gleam flickered in her eyes. "Are they truly alive? Or are you simply seeing what has always been there, hidden from those who refuse to look?"

Shane's brow furrowed. "But how is this possible? And why us?"

Mrs. Eldridge's form seemed to shimmer, becoming less substantial with each passing moment. "Some questions can only be answered by those brave enough to seek the truth. Remember, boys... in this place, history is not just recorded. It breathes."

With those final words, she vanished, leaving the boys alone once more in the oppressive silence of the museum.

Jake's mind reeled, trying to process what they'd just witnessed. He glanced at his friends, seeing his own mix of fear and fascination mirrored in their eyes. Whatever was happening here, it was clear they were in far deeper than they'd ever imagined.

The oppressive silence was shattered by the sharp click of a flashlight beam cutting through the darkness. Jake instinctively pulled Amir and

Shane behind a nearby display case, his heart hammering against his ribs.

"Who's there?" a gruff voice called out, laced with a mixture of wariness and resignation.

Jake exchanged a quick glance with his friends before stepping out, hands raised. "We're... we're just kids. We didn't mean any harm."

The beam lowered, revealing a tall, gaunt figure in a worn security uniform. His deep-set eyes seemed to hold an ocean of unspoken stories as he regarded the boys with a mix of suspicion and concern.

"Henry Thorne," he introduced himself, his voice barely above a whisper. "Night watchman. Though I suspect you boys have seen things no watchman could ever hope to prevent."

Amir stepped forward, curiosity overriding his fear. "Mr. Thorne, what's happening here? The exhibits... they're alive!"

Henry's gaze flickered to the shadows, as if expecting them to leap out at any moment. "Alive? Perhaps. Or perhaps simply awakened from a long slumber." He ran a trembling hand through his thinning hair. "This museum... it holds more than just relics of the past. It holds their essence, their... power."

Jake felt a chill run down his spine. "What do you mean, power?"

Henry's eyes met Jake's, filled with a haunted intensity. "There are artifacts here that should never have been disturbed. I tried to warn them, years ago, but..." He trailed off, his shoulders sagging under an invisible weight.

Shane placed a reassuring hand on Jake's shoulder. "Is there a way to stop it? To put everything back to sleep?"

A humorless chuckle escaped Henry's lips. "If only it were that simple, lad. The genie's out of the bottle now, and it's thirsty for more than just freedom."

As if on cue, a cold draft whispered through the corridor, carrying with it the faintest sound of distant, mocking laughter. Jake felt the hairs on the back of his neck stand up, a primal instinct screaming at him to run.

"It knows you're here," Henry murmured, his flashlight beam dancing erratically across the walls. "And I'm afraid it's taken quite an interest in you boys."

Amir's voice quavered as he asked, "What... what is 'it'?"

Before Henry could answer, the shadows around them seemed to deepen, taking on an almost liquid quality. The air grew thick and oppressive, as if the very atmosphere was closing in around them.

Jake's breath caught in his throat as he saw movement in his peripheral vision - a dark, formless shape slithering along the wall. When he turned to look directly at it, it vanished, only to reappear on the opposite side.

"We need to move," Henry urged, his voice tight with barely contained panic. "Now!"

As they hurried down the corridor, Jake couldn't shake the feeling of unseen eyes boring into his back. The whispers grew louder, a cacophony of indistinct voices that seemed to come from everywhere and nowhere at once.

"What do we do?" Jake asked, trying to keep his voice steady for the sake of his friends.

Henry's response was grim. "We survive. And pray that's enough."

Jake's heart pounded as they rushed through the darkened halls, the whispers growing more insistent with each step. Suddenly, a gust of frigid air swept past them, carrying with it a voice that chilled Jake to his core.

"Blood of my blood," it hissed, seeming to emanate from the very walls. "You've returned."

Jake stumbled, his eyes wide with disbelief. "What... what does that mean?"

Amir grabbed his arm, steadying him. "Jake, what's wrong?"

"That voice," Jake whispered, his face pale. "It sounded like... like my grandmother."

Shane's brow furrowed. "Your grandmother? But she's-"

"Dead," Jake finished. "For ten years now."

Henry's flashlight beam trembled as he turned to face Jake. "Your grandmother... was she by any chance Evelyn Eldridge?"

Jake nodded slowly, a cold dread settling in his stomach. "How did you know?"

"Because," Henry said, his voice heavy with resignation, "Evelyn Eldridge was the last living descendant of Agatha Eldridge, the woman who founded this museum. And if what I fear is true, her blood - your blood - is the key to awakening the entity that's been dormant here for decades."

The air around them seemed to pulse with malevolent energy. Jake felt a tugging sensation, as if invisible tendrils were trying to pull him deeper into the museum's depths.

"We can't let that happen," Amir said firmly, gripping Jake's shoulder. "Whatever this thing is, whatever it wants with Jake, we're not going to let it win."

Shane nodded, his usual jovial demeanor replaced by steely determination. "We're in this together, mate. All the way."

Jake swallowed hard, touched by his friends' loyalty even as fear threatened to overwhelm him. "Thanks, guys. But... what do we do now?"

Henry's flashlight beam settled on a set of ornate double doors at the end of the corridor. "We face it," he said grimly. "In the sanctuary where it's strongest. It's the only way to end this."

As they approached the doors, Jake could feel the malevolent presence growing stronger, a suffocating weight pressing down on him. The whispers coalesced into a single, chilling voice that seemed to reverberate through his very bones.

"Come, child of Eldridge," it crooned. "Embrace your legacy. Embrace me."

Jake's hand trembled as he reached for the door handle. "I'm scared," he admitted, his voice barely above a whisper.

Amir squeezed his shoulder. "We all are. But we're here with you."

"Whatever happens," Shane added, "we face it together."

With a deep breath, Jake pushed open the doors, revealing the cavernous sanctuary beyond. As they stepped inside, the air itself seemed to writhe with shadows, coalescing into a towering, formless entity that loomed over them.

"Welcome home," it hissed, its voice a symphony of terror and seduction. "I've been waiting for you."

Jake's heart hammered in his chest as he faced the Malevolent Entity, its form shifting and writhing like a living nightmare. The air crackled with an otherworldly energy, making the hairs on his arms stand on end.

"We're not here to join you," Jake said, his voice wavering but determined. "We're here to end this."

A chilling laugh echoed through the sanctuary. "Foolish children. You cannot defeat what you do not understand."

Amir's eyes darted around the room, taking in every detail. "The puzzles, Jake," he whispered urgently. "Remember what Agatha said? The key lies in the past."

Jake nodded, his mind racing. "Shane, watch our backs. Amir, help me figure this out."

As Shane stood guard, Jake and Amir moved swiftly from exhibit to exhibit, piecing together clues hidden in the ancient artifacts. The entity's presence grew stronger, shadows lashing out at them like tendrils of darkness.

"Hurry!" Shane called out, barely dodging a spectral attack.

Jake's fingers trembled as he aligned the final piece of the puzzle. "I think I've got it!" he shouted.

Suddenly, the room erupted in a maelstrom of otherworldly energy. The boys huddled together, clinging to each other as the entity's furious screams filled their ears.

"You cannot banish me!" it howled. "I am eternal!"

As the chaos swirled around them, Jake felt a surge of courage. "We're not trying to banish you," he said, his voice growing stronger. "We're setting you free."

With a final, deafening shriek, the entity imploded, leaving behind a profound silence. The boys stood motionless, hardly daring to breathe.

"Is it... over?" Shane whispered.

As if in answer, the first rays of dawn began to filter through the sanctuary's windows. Jake felt a wave of exhaustion wash over him, his legs buckling beneath him.

"We did it," he murmured, tears streaming down his face. "We actually did it."

Amir slumped against a nearby pillar, his face pale and drawn. "I never want to see another museum as long as I live," he said weakly, attempting a smile.

Shane helped Jake to his feet, his own hands shaking. "Let's get out of here," he said, his voice thick with emotion.

As they made their way through the now-quiet halls of the museum, Jake couldn't shake the feeling that they had been irrevocably changed. The weight of their experience hung heavy on their shoulders, a shared burden that would bind them together forever.

"Do you think anyone will believe us?" Amir asked as they approached the exit.

Jake shook his head. "I'm not sure I believe it myself," he admitted. "But I know what we saw, what we felt. That's real enough for me."

As they stepped out into the wan light of dawn, Jake took a deep breath, feeling both utterly drained and strangely alive. The world seemed different now, filled with shadows and mysteries he had never noticed before.

"Whatever happens next," Shane said softly, "we face it together. Just like we did in there."

Jake nodded, grateful for his friends' unwavering support. As they walked away from the museum, he couldn't help but glance back one last time, wondering what other secrets lay hidden behind its imposing facade.

The rusted gates of the Eldridge Historical Museum groaned shut behind them, the sound echoing in the early morning stillness. Jake shuddered involuntarily, his eyes fixed on the ornate iron bars as they clanged into place.

"I can't believe it's over," Amir whispered, his voice hoarse from exhaustion.

Jake turned to his friends, noting the pallor of their faces and the haunted look in their eyes. "Is it really over, though?" he mused, more to himself than to them.

Shane placed a reassuring hand on Jake's shoulder. "We did what we had to do. That thing... it's gone now."

But Jake couldn't shake the nagging feeling that they had only scratched the surface of something much larger and more sinister. He closed his eyes, inhaling deeply. The crisp morning air was a stark contrast to the musty, oppressive atmosphere of the museum.

"What if it comes back?" Amir asked, voicing the fear that had been gnawing at Jake's insides.

Jake opened his eyes, meeting Amir's worried gaze. "Then we'll be ready," he said with more confidence than he felt. "We know what we're up against now."

As they began to walk away, Jake's mind raced with unanswered questions. What was the true nature of the entity they had faced? And why had it chosen them?

"Guys," Shane said, breaking the tense silence, "do you think Mrs. Eldridge knew about all of this?"

Jake frowned, remembering the enigmatic curator's cryptic words. "I think she knew more than she let on. But why didn't she warn us?"

The boys exchanged worried glances, the weight of their shared experience hanging heavily between them. Jake couldn't help but feel that they had stumbled upon something far beyond their understanding, a dark secret that had been waiting centuries to be uncovered.

As they reached the end of the block, Jake turned for one last look at the museum. In the pale light of dawn, it looked almost innocent, its windows reflecting the brightening sky. But Jake knew better now. He knew what lurked in the shadows, waiting.

"Let's go home," he said quietly, his voice laced with a mixture of relief and lingering dread. "But promise me something, both of you."

Amir and Shane nodded; their expressions solemn.

"We stay vigilant," Jake continued, his eyes darting back to the museum. "Whatever we awakened in there... I have a feeling it's not finished with us yet."

As they walked away, Jake couldn't shake the sensation of unseen eyes watching their retreat. The museum may have released them for now, but he feared that their ordeal was far from over. The mysteries that remained unresolved tugged at his mind, a siren call that both terrified and intrigued him.

THE GHOSTLY GUARDIAN

Judy Landon's fingers trembled slightly as she gripped the dry erase marker, the acrid scent of its ink tickling her nostrils. She turned from the whiteboard, its surface a sprawling web of algebraic equations, to face her classroom. Twenty-five pairs of eyes stared back at her, some bright with understanding, others glazed with confusion.

Her gaze swept across the room, a practiced motion honed by years of teaching. But as she reached the third row, her breath caught in her throat. There, sitting quietly at his desk, was Jay.

The marker slipped from her grasp, clattering to the floor. The sound echoed in the sudden silence, drawing curious glances from her students. But Judy couldn't tear her eyes away from the boy.

His features were hauntingly familiar - the same unruly dark hair, the same piercing blue eyes that seemed to look right through her. It was as if Brandon had walked out of her memories and into her classroom.

"Mrs. Landon?" a voice called out, snapping her back to reality. "Are you okay?"

Judy blinked rapidly, forcing a smile onto her face. "Yes, thank you, Emily. I'm fine. Just... lost my grip for a moment."

She bent to retrieve the marker, using the moment to compose herself. As she straightened, she caught Jay's gaze. A chill ran down her spine at the intensity of his stare.

"Now, where were we?" Judy asked, her voice wavering slightly. She turned back to the board, desperately trying to focus on the lesson. But her mind kept drifting, memories of Brandon flooding in like a tidal wave.

She remembered his laughter, the way his eyes would crinkle at the corners when he smiled. The sound of his voice calling "Mom!" as he ran into her arms after school. The weight of his small hand in hers as they walked to the park.

Judy's vision blurred, and she blinked back tears. She couldn't break down, not here, not now. She had to stay strong for her students.

"Mrs. Landon?" It was Jay's voice this time, soft yet somehow filling the room. "Are you sure you're alright?"

She turned, meeting those achingly familiar eyes once more. "I'm fine, Jay. Thank you for asking."

But she wasn't fine. Her heart raced, her palms grew clammy. How could this boy look so much like Brandon? It was impossible, and yet...

Judy took a deep breath, steadying herself. "Let's continue with our lesson, class. Who can tell me the next step in solving this equation?"

As hands shot up around the room, Judy's gaze drifted back to Jay. He wasn't raising his hand, wasn't even looking at the board. His eyes remained fixed on her, watching with an unsettling intensity that sent shivers down her spine.

The fluorescent lights of the teacher's lounge flickered, casting eerie shadows across the worn linoleum floor. Judy slumped into a faded armchair, her fingers trembling as she clutched a lukewarm cup of coffee. The silence in the room was deafening, broken only by the incessant ticking of the wall clock.

Her mind reeled, images of Brandon's final moments flashing before her eyes like a twisted slideshow. The lake, so serene and inviting. His laughter as he splashed in the shallows. Then, the heart-stopping moment when she turned away, just for a second...

Judy's breath hitched. "I should have been watching," she whispered, her voice cracking. "If only I'd—"

The sudden creak of the door made her jolt, coffee sloshing over her fingers. She looked up, expecting to see a colleague, but instead found herself staring into those hauntingly familiar blue eyes.

Jay stood in the doorway, his pale face seeming to glow in the dim light. He moved with an unnatural grace, his footsteps making no sound as he approached.

"Mrs. Landon," he said, his voice soft yet penetrating. "I hope I'm not disturbing you."

A chill raced down Judy's spine. How had he entered so silently? And why was he here, in the teacher's lounge of all places?

"Jay," she managed, forcing a smile that felt brittle on her face. "What are you doing here? Students aren't allowed in this area."

He tilted his head, a knowing smile playing at the corners of his mouth. "I thought you might need some company," he replied, his gaze never wavering from hers.

Judy's heart thundered in her chest. There was something in his eyes, something old and wise that had no place in a child's face. She opened her mouth to speak, but the words caught in her throat. What could she possibly say to this boy who looked so much like her lost son?

Judy's fingers trembled as she set down her coffee mug, the ceramic clinking against the worn tabletop. Jay slid into the chair across from her, his movements fluid and unnaturally graceful.

"You know," Jay began, his voice carrying a weight beyond his years, "Brandon always loved the smell of coffee. He'd sneak sips from your mug when you weren't looking."

Judy's breath caught. "How... how could you possibly know that?" she whispered, her eyes widening in disbelief.

Jay's lips curved into a sad smile. "I know a lot of things, Mrs. Landon. Like how you used to sing 'You Are My Sunshine' to Brandon every night before bed. Or how you both loved to watch the fireflies on summer evenings from the porch swing."

Each word was a dagger to Judy's heart, memories flooding back with painful clarity. Her mind reeled, searching for any logical explanation. "Did... did someone tell you these things?" she asked, her voice quavering.

Jay shook his head slowly. "No one told me. I just know."

Judy's hands gripped the edge of the table, her knuckles turning white. "This isn't possible," she murmured, more to herself than to Jay.

As Jay opened his mouth to speak again, Judy abruptly stood, her chair screeching against the linoleum. "I... I need to go," she stammered, her heart racing. Without another word, she rushed from the lounge, leaving a bewildered Jay behind.

Her footsteps echoed in the empty hallway as she made her way towards the library, her mind a whirlwind of confusion and fear. *Karen,* she thought desperately. *Karen will know what to make of this.*

Pushing through the library doors, Judy spotted Karen's vibrant red hair behind the circulation desk. She approached, trying to steady her breathing.

"Karen," Judy said, her voice barely above a whisper. "I need your help. It's... it's about something unusual. Something that might be... supernatural."

Karen looked up, her green eyes filled with concern. "Judy? What's wrong?"

Judy glanced around, ensuring they were alone. "It's about one of my students," she began, her words tumbling out in a rush. "He knows things... things he couldn't possibly know. About my son, about me. It's as if... as if he's not just a normal boy."

Karen's expression shifted from concern to intrigue. "Tell me everything," she said softly, leaning in closer.

As Judy recounted her encounters with Jay, she felt a mix of relief and apprehension. Would Karen think she was losing her mind? Or could she possibly shed light on this inexplicable situation?

Karen's emerald eyes widened as she listened, her slender fingers drumming thoughtfully on the worn oak desk. The musty scent of old books enveloped them, providing an oddly comforting backdrop to Judy's tale of the impossible.

"I believe you, Judy," Karen said, her voice a soothing balm to Judy's frayed nerves. "There are more things in heaven and earth than most people realize. Come with me."

They weaved through towering shelves, Karen's fiery hair a beacon in the dim light. She pulled out tome after tome, their leather bindings creaking as she stacked them on a secluded table.

"These texts speak of spirits unable to move on," Karen explained, her finger tracing faded illustrations of spectral figures. "Sometimes, they return with unfinished business."

Judy's heart raced as she scanned the pages. "But why would he appear as a student? Why not just... himself?"

Karen's brow furrowed. "Perhaps to protect you, to stay close without arousing suspicion."

As they delved deeper, Judy's hands trembled over a passage about guardian spirits. The words blurred as tears welled in her eyes.

"Oh God," she whispered, a chill running down her spine. "It's Brandon, isn't it? He's come back to me."

Karen placed a comforting hand on Judy's shoulder. "It seems likely. But Judy, if it is him, why has he returned now?"

Judy's mind reeled, hope and horror warring within her. "To protect me? But from what?"

"That," Karen said softly, "is what we need to find out."

The incessant ticking of the alarm clock pierced the pre-dawn gloom, each second hammering home the significance of the day. Judy's eyes snapped open, her heart already racing. She lay motionless, the weight of dread pressing her into the mattress.

Pale light seeped through the curtains as Judy went through her morning routine, her movements mechanical and distant. The mirror reflected a face etched with worry, dark circles underlining eyes that darted nervously about the room.

"Just another day," Judy whispered to her reflection, her trembling hands smoothing non-existent wrinkles from her blouse. "You can do this."

As she descended the stairs, a framed photo of Brandon caught her eye. His frozen smile sent a jolt through her, a bittersweet reminder of what she'd lost and what had impossibly returned.

The drive to school was a blur of autumn colors and racing thoughts. Judy gripped the steering wheel, her knuckles white.

"Why today?" she murmured, glancing at the passenger seat where Jay – no, Brandon – had sat just yesterday. "Why did you come back to save me on this day of all days?"

The school parking lot loomed ahead, a sea of cars glinting in the morning sun. Judy's breath caught as she spotted Jay waiting by the entrance, his pale face a beacon amidst the bustle of arriving students.

She approached him, her steps faltering. "Good morning, Jay," she said, her voice barely above a whisper.

Jay's piercing blue eyes met hers, filled with an impossible mixture of youth and ancient wisdom. "Good morning, Mrs. Landon," he replied, his voice soft yet charged with unspoken meaning. "Please, be careful today."

Judy's heart clenched. "I... I will," she managed, fighting the urge to embrace him, to never let go.

As she turned to enter the building, Jay's words echoed in her mind, a haunting reminder of the danger that lurked in the hours ahead.

The screech of tires tore through the air, shattering the mundane hum of traffic. Judy's eyes widened in terror as she saw the car barreling towards her, its red paint gleaming like fresh blood in the afternoon sun. Time seemed to slow, stretching each second into an eternity.

Suddenly, a shimmer of pale light coalesced before her. Jay materialized, his form translucent and glowing with an otherworldly aura. His blue eyes, so achingly familiar, locked onto hers with fierce determination.

"Mom!" he cried, his voice echoing as if from a great distance.

With supernatural speed, Jay's spectral hands pressed against Judy's shoulders, propelling her backwards. She felt a rush of cold air as she stumbled onto the sidewalk, her heart pounding in her chest.

The car roared past, passing harmlessly through Jay's ethereal form. Judy watched in awe as his essence rippled like smoke in the vehicle's wake, reforming slowly as the danger passed.

"Brandon," Judy whispered, her voice choked with emotion. "It really is you."

Jay turned to her, a sad smile playing on his ghostly lips. "I couldn't let you die, Mom. Not like this."

Tears streamed down Judy's face as she reached out, her fingers passing through Jay's translucent cheek. "I've missed you so much," she sobbed. "Please, don't go."

Jay's form began to flicker, growing fainter with each passing moment. "I have to," he said softly. "My task is done. But remember, I'll always love you."

Judy's heart ached as she watched her son's spirit fade away, leaving behind only a lingering warmth in the air. She stood there, trembling, as the reality of what had just transpired washed over her.

"Thank you," she whispered to the empty space where Jay had been, her words carried away by the gentle breeze. The world around her slowly came back into focus – the honking of cars, the chatter of passersby – but Judy remained rooted to the spot, her mind reeling from the miraculous intervention and the bittersweet reunion.

Judy's fingers traced the cool marble of Brandon's headstone, feeling the familiar curves of his name etched into the surface. The cemetery was quiet, save for the rustle of leaves in the autumn breeze. She placed a small, smooth stone atop the grave marker, a gesture that had become ritual over the years.

"I understand now, sweetheart," Judy murmured, her voice barely above a whisper. "You've been watching over me all this time."

She closed her eyes, recalling Jay's – Brandon's – ethereal form dissolving into the air. The memory, once tinged with horror, now filled her with a bittersweet warmth.

"Ms. Landon?" A small voice broke through her reverie.

Judy turned to see one of her students, Emma, standing a few feet away, clutching a bouquet of wildflowers.

"Emma, what are you doing here?" Judy asked, quickly wiping away a stray tear.

The girl shuffled her feet. "My grandpa's buried here. I saw you and... are you okay?"

Judy managed a warm smile. "I'm better than okay, Emma. I'm grateful."

Emma tilted her head, curious. "For what?"

"For the reminder that love... true love... it doesn't end. Not really." Judy's gaze drifted back to Brandon's headstone. "It just changes form."

"Like a caterpillar turning into a butterfly?" Emma asked, her eyes wide with innocent wisdom.

Judy chuckled softly. "Exactly like that. Now, why don't you tell me about your grandpa?"

As Emma launched into a story about her grandfather's famous apple pie, Judy felt a weight lift from her shoulders. She would always miss Brandon, but now she knew – truly knew – that their bond transcended death itself. With each passing moment, each life touched, she would honor his memory by living fully, carrying his love forward into the world.

The autumn sun dipped lower on the horizon, casting long shadows across the cemetery. But for Judy, the world seemed brighter than it had in years, illuminated by the unbreakable connection between a mother and her child – a love that even death couldn't diminish.

LEFT IN THE PAST

The blank page mocks me, its emptiness a void threatening to swallow my dreams. My fingers hover over the keyboard, trembling slightly. I've been sitting here for hours, but the words refuse to come.

"Just write something," I mutter to myself, running a hand through my unruly hair. "Anything."

But my mind is a maelstrom of doubt and frustration. The cramped walls of my tiny apartment press in, suffocating. Outside, the ceaseless hum of New York City traffic drones on, indifferent to my struggle.

I sigh heavily, slumping in my chair. The weight of expectation - my own, my family's - crushes down upon me. Am I truly meant to be a writer, or am I just deluding myself?

My gaze drifts to the antique typewriter perched on the corner of my desk, a relic from a bygone era. Its presence comforts me somehow, a tangible link to the past I so often lose myself in.

"What stories could you tell?" I whisper to it, fingers tracing the worn keys.

Exhaustion tugs at me, pulling my eyelids down. I fight it, but it's a losing battle. As consciousness slips away, fragments of dreams begin to form...

Skyscrapers morph into gas-lit street lamps. The blare of car horns fades to the clip-clop of horses' hooves. Whispers from the past grow louder, becoming a cacophony of voices I can't quite understand.

I jolt awake with a gasp, heart pounding. But something is wrong. The familiar clutter of my apartment has vanished, replaced by...

"Where am I?" My voice sounds strange, muffled by the stillness.

Dim light filters through heavy curtains, illuminating unfamiliar surroundings. The air is thick, musty - redolent with the scents of aged wood and dust. An antique writing desk stands in the corner, its surface marred by ink stains.

Fear creeps up my spine as I struggle to make sense of what I'm seeing. This can't be real. It has to be a dream, doesn't it?

But the floorboards creak ominously beneath my feet as I stand. The chill air raises goosebumps on my skin.

Everything feels too solid, too present to be a mere figment of my imagination.

"Hello?" I call out hesitantly, my words swallowed by the oppressive silence. "Is anyone there?"

Only the faint ticking of an unseen clock answers me.

I stumble to the window, yanking open the heavy curtains. Sunlight floods in, momentarily blinding me. As my vision clears, I stare out in disbelief.

The New York I know is gone. In its place, a sepia-toned world unfolds before me - horse-drawn carriages clattering down cobblestone streets, women in long skirts and men in bowler hats hurrying past.

"No," I whisper, pressing my hand against the cool glass. "This can't be happening."

But the evidence is undeniable. Somehow, impossibly, I've traveled back to 1918.

Fear wars with an irrepressible curiosity within me. I've always been drawn to the past, but this...this is beyond anything I could have imagined.

"Get it together, Jesse," I mutter, running a shaky hand through my hair. "You need to figure this out."

My reflection in the window catches my eye - same unruly dark hair, same brown eyes wide with shock. At least I still look like myself.

The urge to explore, to see this world I've only read about, is overwhelming. Before I can talk myself out of it, I'm heading for the door.

"Just a quick look," I promise myself. "Then I'll come back and...and figure out how to get home."

The floorboards creak ominously under my feet as I step into the hallway. Each sound seems magnified in the eerie quiet, as if the very air is holding its breath.

The dusty hallway leads me to a small study, its shelves lined with leather-bound books and curious artifacts. My writer's instinct kicks in, urging me to explore, to uncover the stories hidden within these walls.

As I run my fingers along the spines of the books, a drawer in the corner desk catches my eye. It's slightly ajar, as if inviting me to peek inside. I hesitate, my conscience warring with my curiosity.

"Just one look," I murmur, pulling it open.

The drawer's contents are unremarkable at first - old papers, a few faded receipts. But as I shuffle through them, my breath catches in my throat. There, nestled among the detritus of a bygone era, is a photograph.

My hands tremble as I lift it to the light. The face staring back at me is eerily familiar - my own features, but not quite. The eyes hold a wisdom beyond their years, a haunting depth that sends a chill down my spine.

"Impossible," I whisper, but the resemblance is undeniable.

A floorboard creaks behind me, and I whirl around, my heart pounding. An older man stands in the doorway, his piercing blue eyes fixed on me with an intensity that makes me want to shrink away.

"I've been expecting you, Jesse," he says, his voice deep and resonant.

I swallow hard, my mind reeling. "How do you know my name?"

A sad smile plays at the corners of his mouth. "I'm Joseph Hubart. Your great-grandfather."

The photograph slips from my fingers, clattering to the floor. "But that's not... I mean, how can you...?"

Joseph's gaze softens. "I know you have questions. Come, let's talk over tea. There's much to discuss."

As I follow him out of the study, a sense of foreboding settles over me. What secrets lie hidden in the depths of those knowing eyes?

The days blur together, each one a tapestry woven from Joseph's stories. I find myself drawn inexorably into the shadowy recesses of our family's past, hanging on every word that falls from his lips.

"The Hubart line has always walked a razor's edge," Joseph murmurs one evening, his eyes distant. "Between light and dark, sanity and madness."

I lean forward, my tea growing cold. "What do you mean?"

He sighs, a heavy sound that seems to carry the weight of generations. "There are... choices we must make. Sacrifices."

A chill runs down my spine. "What kind of sacrifices?"

Joseph's gaze snaps to mine, piercing in its intensity. "Some things are better left unsaid, my boy."

The silence that follows is thick with unspoken truths. I can feel them pressing against my skin, a suffocating presence that threatens to consume me.

"Tell me," I whisper, my voice hoarse.

But Joseph only shakes his head, his fingers trembling as he reaches for his teacup. The tension in the room is palpable, a living thing that coils around us both.

As night falls, I lie awake in the unfamiliar bed, Joseph's words echoing in my mind. What secrets is he guarding? And why do I feel an overwhelming sense of dread every time I look into his eyes?

On the third day, something shifts. Joseph's demeanor changes, an urgency lacing his words that wasn't there before.

"Jesse," he says, gripping my arm with surprising strength. "You must listen carefully. Our ancestors... they left warnings. Prophecies."

My heart races. "About what?"

"Choices," he whispers, his eyes wild. "Choices that could change everything. The very fabric of time itself."

I swallow hard, fear clawing at my throat. "I don't understand."

Joseph's voice drops to a harsh whisper. "You will. But you must be prepared. The path ahead is treacherous, and one misstep could doom us all."

As he speaks, the room seems to darken, shadows creeping in from the corners. I can feel the weight of destiny pressing down on me, suffocating in its intensity.

"What do I need to do?" I ask, my voice barely audible.

Joseph's grip tightens, his eyes boring into mine. "Remember, Jesse. Remember and beware. The choices you make will ripple through time, shaping not just your fate, but the fate of our entire lineage."

A chill runs through me, and I know with terrifying certainty that nothing will ever be the same again.

The weight of Joseph's words presses down on me, each syllable a leaden weight upon my chest. His tales swirl in my mind, a maelstrom of fragmented prophecies and dire warnings. I close my eyes, trying to make sense of it all, but the darkness behind my lids only amplifies the echoes of his voice.

"The choices you make will ripple through time," I murmur, tasting the bitterness of fate on my tongue.

My eyes snap open. The sepia-toned world of 1918 has vanished, replaced by the harsh fluorescent glare of my cramped New York apartment. The abrupt transition leaves me reeling, my heart pounding against my ribs like a caged animal.

"Joseph?" I call out, my voice hoarse and unfamiliar.

Only the distant wail of sirens answers me. I stumble to the window, pressing my forehead against the cool glass. The city sprawls before me, a concrete jungle so far removed from the cobblestone streets I'd just been walking.

"Was it just a dream?" I whisper, but the vivid memories cling to me like a shroud.

I can still smell the musty scent of Joseph's home, still feel the weight of his hand on my arm. The urgency in his eyes haunts me, a spectral presence in the corners of my vision.

My gaze falls on the blank page still sitting on my desk. The cursor blinks accusingly, a stark reminder of my writer's block. But now, words threaten to spill forth, dark and portentous.

"What have I uncovered?" I ask the empty room. "And what am I supposed to do with this knowledge?"

The city offers no answers, its cacophony a jarring counterpoint to the rhythmic cadence of Joseph's warnings still echoing in my mind. I sink into my chair, overwhelmed by the sense that I stand at a crossroads, the fate of generations hanging in the balance of my next move.

With trembling hands, I reach for the leather-bound journal on my nightstand. Joseph's journal. Its presence feels like an anchor, tethering me to a past I'm only beginning to understand.

I flip it open, the yellowed pages crackling beneath my fingertips. Joseph's elegant script dances across the paper, a stark contrast to the chilling words it conveys:

"The shadow that haunts us is no mere figment, dear descendant. It is a malevolence that has stalked our bloodline for centuries, patient and insidious."

My breath catches in my throat. "Bloodline?" I murmur, a chill creeping up my spine.

As I delve deeper into the journal, fragments of suppressed memories flicker to life. A childhood nightmare of glowing red eyes. The inexplicable dread that would overcome me in certain rooms of my grandmother's house. The whispers I'd always attributed to an overactive imagination.

"It wasn't imagination at all," I realize, my voice barely a whisper. "It was real. All of it."

The truth crashes over me like a wave of ice water. Our family isn't just haunted by the past – we're cursed by something far more tangible and terrifying.

Suddenly, the shadows in my apartment seem to lengthen, reaching for me with inky tendrils. The air grows thick, oppressive. In the corner of my eye, I catch a flicker of movement, gone before I can focus on it.

"No," I breathe, clutching the journal to my chest. "I won't let you win."

Desperation fuels me as I tear through my bookshelves, pulling out every tome on the occult I can find. The whispers grow louder, a sinister chant that threatens to drown out my thoughts.

"I need help," I mutter, fumbling for my phone. "Someone who understands this darkness."

As I dial the number of an acquaintance versed in the arcane, I can't shake the feeling that I've set something in motion – a battle that's been brewing for generations, with my soul as the prize.

The room spins, shadows dancing at the edges of my vision. I grip the edge of my desk, knuckles white, trying to anchor myself to reality.

"You cannot win," a voice hisses in my mind, cold and ancient. "Your family's blood is mine."

I squeeze my eyes shut, forcing out a ragged breath. "No," I growl, more to myself than the entity. "I won't let you break me."

Opening my eyes, I fumble for a pen, scrawling furiously in my notebook. The words flow like a fever dream, a jumble of half-remembered stories and cryptic warnings from Joseph's journal.

A chill runs down my spine as I realize the entity is watching, always watching. Its presence weighs on me, a suffocating blanket of malevolence.

"Why us?" I demand, my voice cracking. "Why our family?"

Laughter echoes in my skull, mocking and cruel. "Why not? Your fear... it sustains me."

I slam my fist on the desk, anger flaring. "I'm not afraid of you!"

"Aren't you, Jesse?" it purrs. The shadows coalesce, forming a vaguely humanoid shape with burning red eyes. "I've tasted your nightmares. Your doubts. Your failures."

My heart races, but I force myself to stand, facing the entity. "You don't know me," I spit out. "You don't know what I'm capable of."

It lunges forward, and suddenly I'm falling, tumbling through a void of memories not my own. Glimpses of ancestors long dead, their faces contorted in terror. I see Joseph, his eyes haunted as he scribbles in his journal.

"I am your legacy," the entity whispers. "Your destiny."

But as I plummet through time and space, something shifts. A warmth blooms in my chest, a connection to those who came before. Their strength, their resilience – it flows through me.

"No," I say, my voice steadier now. "You're just a parasite. And I'm going to end this. Here. Now."

The void shatters, and I find myself back in my apartment, gasping for air. The entity looms before me, its form flickering between shadow and substance.

"You cannot banish me," it snarls. "I am eternal."

I straighten my shoulders, drawing on a well of courage I didn't know I possessed. "Maybe. But I can fight you. And I will. For my family. For myself."

As we face off, the air crackles with tension. This is more than just a battle for survival – it's a reckoning generations in the making. And I refuse to let my family's story end in darkness.

I close my eyes, drawing deep from the well of ancestral knowledge that now flows through me. The entity's presence presses against my mind, a suffocating weight of malice and hunger.

"You're nothing," it hisses. "A speck in the vastness of time."

I open my eyes, meeting its burning gaze. "I am everything my ancestors fought for," I say, my voice barely above a whisper. "Their hopes. Their dreams. Their defiance."

With trembling hands, I reach for the tattered journal – Joseph's journal – on my desk. The entity recoils as I open it, the pages humming with a power I can't fully comprehend.

"What are you doing?" it demands, a note of uncertainty creeping into its voice.

I begin to read, my great-grandfather's words tumbling from my lips in a language I shouldn't know. The room darkens, shadows writhing on the walls. I feel a tearing sensation, as if my very essence is being pulled apart.

"Stop!" the entity shrieks, its form contorting grotesquely.

But I can't stop. I won't stop. Even as pain lances through every fiber of my being, I press on, the cadence of the ancient words building to a crescendo.

"This ends now," I grit out, my vision blurring. "With me."

A blinding light erupts from the journal, engulfing us both. I feel myself fading, dissolving into the ether. But as darkness claims me, I catch a glimpse of sunlight breaking through storm clouds. And I know, with my last breath, that it's finally over.

THE MIRROR'S WHISPER

The ancient key scraped in the lock, echoing through the empty halls of the old Victorian house. Richard Fields held his breath as the heavy oak door creaked open, revealing a dimly lit foyer shrouded in dust and shadows.

"Oh, Richard, isn't it magnificent?" Samantha Fields stepped inside, her green eyes sparkling with excitement. "Just look at that chandelier!"

Richard's gaze followed his mother's outstretched hand to the tarnished crystal fixture hanging overhead. Cobwebs draped from its delicate arms like gossamer curtains. A chill ran down his spine as he crossed the threshold.

"It's... something," he muttered, his eyes darting to the dark corners of the room. The floorboards groaned beneath his feet, and he couldn't shake the feeling of being watched.

Samantha's heels clicked on the hardwood as she moved further inside. "I can already picture how cozy this place will be once we get it fixed up. What do you think, honey?"

Richard forced a smile. "Yeah, Mom. It'll be great." But his thoughts raced: *Why does it feel so... wrong?*

"Why don't you go pick out your room while I start unpacking?" Samantha suggested, her voice brimming with enthusiasm.

Nodding, Richard hefted his backpack and began climbing the creaking stairs. Each step seemed to whisper secrets, and the faded wallpaper peeled away from the walls like withered skin.

At the top of the landing, a long hallway stretched before him, lined with closed doors. Richard's hand hesitated on each doorknob, his curiosity warring with an inexplicable sense of dread.

Finally, he pushed open the last door on the right. The room beyond was spacious, with high ceilings and large windows. But it was the mirror that commanded his attention.

Standing six feet tall, its ornate golden frame glinted in the fading sunlight. Richard approached it cautiously, his reflection growing clearer with each step.

"Whoa," he breathed, reaching out to touch the cool glass. "This thing's massive."

As his fingers made contact, a jolt of electricity seemed to pass through him. Richard stumbled back, his heart racing. "What the hell?"

He peered closer at the mirror, searching for any sign of what had caused the strange sensation. But all he saw was his own reflection, brown eyes wide with a mix of fear and fascination.

"Everything okay up there?" Samantha called from downstairs.

Richard swallowed hard. "Yeah, Mom. Just checking out my room."

But as he turned away, he couldn't shake the feeling that something in the mirror was still watching him, waiting.

Richard's eyes darted back to the mirror, his breath catching in his throat. For a split second, he saw it—a face, not his own, peering out from the glass. Gaunt and sorrowful, with hollow eyes that seemed to bore into his soul.

"What the—" he gasped, stumbling backward. His heart hammered against his ribs as he blinked rapidly, trying to make sense of what he'd seen. But the image was gone, leaving only his own startled reflection staring back at him.

"It's just my imagination," Richard muttered, running a hand through his dark hair. "Old houses play tricks on you, that's all." Yet he couldn't shake the chill that ran down his spine, or the nagging feeling that what he'd seen was more than a trick of the light.

Days passed, and Richard found himself constantly drawn back to the mirror, studying it intently for any sign of the mysterious figure. He'd almost convinced himself it had been nothing more than a product of an overactive imagination when the storm hit.

Thunder rumbled ominously outside as Richard sat at his desk, algebra textbook open before him. Lightning flashed, illuminating his room in stark white for a moment before plunging it back into shadow.

"Focus, Richard," he muttered to himself, tapping his pencil against the paper. "You can't let some creepy old mirror distract you from—"

A flicker of movement caught his eye, and Richard's head snapped up. The mirror seemed to shimmer, an otherworldly glow emanating from its surface. He rose slowly, drawn towards it as if by an invisible force.

"This isn't possible," he whispered, his voice barely audible over the pounding rain. But as he approached, the glow intensified, pulsing like a heartbeat. Richard's reflection wavered and distorted, the glass seeming to ripple like water.

His hand reached out, trembling slightly. "What are you trying to show me?"

As his fingers brushed the cool surface, a jolt of energy surged through him, and the world around Richard seemed to fade away. All that existed was the mirror, and the secrets it held within its shimmering depths.

Richard's breath caught in his throat as the mirror's surface rippled once more, revealing a figure standing beside his reflection. A boy, no older than twelve, with dirty blonde hair and piercing blue eyes that seemed to bore into Richard's soul. The boy's tattered clothing hung loosely on his thin frame, a stark contrast to Richard's modern jeans and t-shirt.

"Who... who are you?" Richard whispered, his voice barely audible over the storm raging outside.

The spectral boy's lips moved, but no sound came out. His eyes, filled with an eternal sadness, pleaded silently for understanding.

Richard's mind raced, trying to process what he was seeing. "This can't be real," he muttered, running a hand through his dark hair. "I must be dreaming."

But the boy in the mirror remained, his ghostly form unwavering. Richard noticed how the boy's threadbare shirt and patched trousers seemed to belong to another era entirely.

"Are you... from the past?" Richard asked, his curiosity overriding his fear.

The boy nodded slowly, a flicker of hope crossing his sorrowful features.

Richard's heart pounded in his chest. "I'm Richard," he said, pressing his palm against the glass. "Can you tell me your name?"

The boy's lips moved again, and this time, Richard could almost hear a whisper: "Josiah."

A chill ran down Richard's spine, but excitement bubbled up within him. He had always loved solving puzzles, and now a mystery beyond his wildest dreams stood before him.

"Josiah," Richard repeated, his brown eyes intense with determination. "I don't know how, but I'm going to help you. I promise."

As the storm raged on, Richard grabbed a notebook and began scribbling furiously. Questions, theories, and observations filled the pages as he glanced between his notes and the mirror, where Josiah's ghostly form remained.

"I'll figure this out," Richard muttered, more to himself than to Josiah. "Whatever happened to you, whatever this curse is... I'll find the truth."

Richard's fingers trembled as he pried open the ancient leather-bound journal, its musty scent filling his nostrils. Dust motes danced in the pale shaft of moonlight streaming through his bedroom window, casting eerie shadows across the yellowed pages.

"July 15, 1886," he read aloud, his voice barely above a whisper. "Another servant vanished today. That makes three this month. The master grows more agitated, his temper flaring like hellfire. I fear a darkness has taken hold of this house..."

A floorboard creaked behind him, and Richard whirled around, heart pounding. Nothing but empty air. He swallowed hard, turning back to the diary.

"Mom!" he called out, excitement overriding his unease. "Mom, you've got to see this!"

Samantha's footsteps echoed in the hallway before she appeared in the doorway, concern etched on her face. "What is it, honey? It's nearly midnight."

Richard held up the journal, his brown eyes gleaming. "I found this hidden behind a loose panel. It talks about disappearances, Mom. Something terrible happened here."

Samantha's brow furrowed as she took the book, thumbing through its brittle pages. "Richard, this is probably just some old fiction someone left behind. You shouldn't take it so seriously."

"But Mom, it explains everything! The weird noises, the cold spots, even that boy I saw in the—"

A loud crash from downstairs cut him off. Richard jumped to his feet, but Samantha placed a calming hand on his shoulder.

"It's just the wind, sweetheart. This old house settles in strange ways."

Richard shook his head vehemently. "No, Mom, it's more than that. Can't you feel it? There's something... wrong here."

Samantha sighed, running a hand through her wavy brown hair. "Richard, I know the move has been hard on you, but you can't let your imagination run wild like this. There are no ghosts, no curses. Just a beautiful old house that needs some TLC."

As if in response to her words, the lights in Richard's room flickered ominously. A chill swept through the air, raising goosebumps on his arms.

"Did you see that?" Richard insisted, gesturing wildly. "Mom, please, you have to believe me!"

Samantha's green eyes softened with sympathy. "Honey, old wiring can cause all sorts of—"

Before she could finish, Richard's desk lamp sailed across the room, shattering against the far wall. Samantha's eyes widened in shock, but she quickly composed herself.

"It... it must have been unbalanced," she stammered, her usual confidence wavering. "Let's get this cleaned up and get some sleep. Things will look clearer in the morning."

As Samantha left to fetch a broom, Richard turned back to the mirror, frustration etched across his young face. "She doesn't understand," he whispered to Josiah's faint reflection. "But I won't give up. I'll find a way to help you, no matter what it takes."

Richard's fingers trembled as he gripped the edge of his desk, knuckles turning white. The weight of isolation pressed down on him, heavier than the dusty air of the old house. He glanced at the mirror, catching a fleeting glimpse of Josiah's sorrowful eyes.

"I can't keep living like this," Richard muttered, running a hand through his dark hair. "No one believes me, but I know what I've seen. What I've felt."

He straightened, a spark of determination igniting in his brown eyes. "If no one else will help, then I'll do it myself."

Richard's gaze swept across his room, landing on the crumbling spines of the old diaries he'd discovered. "There has to be more," he whispered. "Something I've missed."

With renewed purpose, Richard strode out of his room, his footsteps echoing through the silent house. The floorboards creaked beneath him as he approached the attic stairs, each step feeling like a decision that couldn't be undone.

As he reached for the attic door, a chill ran down his spine. "This is crazy," he thought, his hand hovering over the knob. "But what choice do I have?"

The door groaned as Richard pushed it open, revealing a space thick with cobwebs and forgotten memories. Dust motes danced in the weak light filtering through a grimy window. Richard's eyes darted around, searching for anything out of place.

"Come on," he muttered, "there has to be something here."

His fingers traced along shelves and boxes, leaving trails in the dust. Suddenly, a glint caught his eye. Wedged between two rotting floorboards was a scrap of yellowed paper.

Richard's heart raced as he carefully extracted it. Faded ink formed unfamiliar symbols and words. "An incantation?" he whispered, a mix of excitement and fear coursing through him.

As he studied the strange writing, Richard felt a presence behind him. He turned, half-expecting to see Josiah, but found only shadows.

"Is this it?" Richard asked the empty attic. "Is this how I can help you, Josiah?"

The paper seemed to pulse with an otherworldly energy in his hands. Richard swallowed hard, torn between hope and terror.

"I don't know if this is the right thing to do," he said aloud, his voice shaky. "But I can't just leave you trapped like this. Whatever happens... I have to try."

With the incantation clutched tightly in his fist, Richard made his way back to his room, each step feeling like a march toward an uncertain destiny.

Richard stood before the towering mirror, its ornate frame looming over him like a silent sentinel. His reflection stared back, pale and determined, the scrap of paper trembling in his outstretched hand. The room seemed to hold its breath, shadows deepening in the corners as if retreating from what was about to unfold.

"Okay, Josiah," Richard whispered, his voice barely audible. "I hope this works."

He began to recite the incantation, the unfamiliar words feeling heavy on his tongue. As he spoke, the air grew thick, pressing against him like an invisible force.

"Animae liberantur, portae aperiuntur..."

The mirror's surface rippled, distorting Richard's reflection. His heart pounded, but he pressed on, voice growing stronger with each syllable.

"Vincula franguntur, spiritus emergunt!"

A low hum filled the room, vibrating through Richard's bones. The mirror's glass began to glow, pulsing with an eerie, blue-white light.

"It's happening," Richard gasped, eyes wide. "Josiah, can you hear me?"

The light intensified, forcing Richard to squint. Through the glare, he saw a familiar figure taking shape – Josiah, his tattered clothes and sorrowful eyes as vivid as ever.

"Richard," Josiah's voice echoed, seeming to come from everywhere at once. "You've done it. The barrier... it's breaking."

A deafening crack split the air. Richard stumbled backward as the mirror's surface fractured, spider-web cracks racing across its expanse. Energy surged outward in a blinding flash, knocking him to the floor.

When Richard's vision cleared, he found himself in a transformed room. Where the imposing mirror once stood, there was now only an empty space on the wall. And there, bathed in a soft, otherworldly glow, stood Josiah.

The ghostly boy's form was different now – no longer trapped behind glass, but fully present. A smile, tinged with both joy and sadness, played across his lips.

"You've freed me," Josiah said, his voice carrying the weight of centuries. "After all this time..."

Richard slowly got to his feet, awe and disbelief warring within him. "Are you... really here?"

Josiah nodded, his form already beginning to fade. "Yes, but not for long. The curse is broken, and I can finally rest."

"Wait!" Richard cried, reaching out. "There's so much I want to ask you, to understand!"

Josiah's smile grew wistful. "Some mysteries are meant to remain unsolved, Richard. But know this – your kindness and courage have brought peace to a tormented soul. Thank you."

With those words, Josiah's form dissipated like mist in sunlight. The oppressive atmosphere that had permeated the house lifted, leaving behind a profound silence.

Richard stood alone in the room, staring at the blank wall where the mirror had been. A mix of emotions washed over him – relief, wonder, and a lingering unease at the power he had just wielded.

"Goodbye, Josiah," he whispered to the empty air, feeling both triumphant and somehow bereft.

The silence in the room pressed against Richard's eardrums, a stark contrast to the supernatural cacophony that had filled it moments before. Moonlight streamed through the window, casting long shadows across the floor where the mirror once stood. Richard's fingers twitched, half-expecting to feel the cold glass beneath them.

"It's over," he murmured, his voice sounding unnaturally loud in the quiet. "It's really over."

He paced the length of the room, his footsteps echoing hollowly. Each step felt like an affirmation of the solidity of his world, now jarringly mundane after the extraordinary events he'd just experienced.

Richard paused at the window, staring out at the peaceful Kansas night. "How can everything look so... normal?" he wondered aloud. "When nothing will ever be normal again?"

His reflection in the window pane caught his eye – familiar brown eyes now carrying a weight they hadn't before. Richard's mind raced, grappling with the implications of what he'd witnessed and done.

"Mom will never believe this," he said, a hint of bitter laughter in his voice. "No one will."

The thought of trying to explain sent a wave of isolation washing over him. Richard's shoulders slumped as he turned back to face the empty room.

"I helped a ghost find peace," he said, testing the words. They sounded ridiculous, even to his own ears. "I shattered a curse. I... changed reality."

Richard's gaze fell on the ancient incantation, still clutched in his trembling hand. He carefully folded the paper, tucking it into his pocket.

"What else is out there?" he whispered, a mix of fear and exhilaration coursing through him. "If this was real, what other impossibilities are waiting to be discovered?"

As the adrenaline began to fade, exhaustion settled over Richard like a heavy blanket. He sank onto his bed, mind still whirling.

"Everything's different now," he murmured, staring at his hands. "I'm different. How do I just... go back to normal life after this?"

The question hung in the air, unanswered. Richard lay back, knowing sleep would be elusive tonight. The memory of Josiah's grateful smile flickered through his mind, a bittersweet reminder of the extraordinary experience that now set him apart from everyone else in his life.

As the night deepened, Richard's thoughts continued to churn, caught between wonder at what he'd accomplished and uncertainty about what it meant for his future. The world had expanded beyond what he'd ever imagined, leaving him both thrilled and unnerved by the possibilities that now stretched before him.

THE THIRTEENTH HOUR

Megan's breath billowed in wispy clouds as she trudged up the winding gravel driveway, each crunch beneath her feet echoing in the oppressive silence. The dilapidated mansion loomed before her, its weathered facade a patchwork of peeling paint and rotting wood. Shadows danced in the hollow windows, seeming to watch her approach with malevolent interest.

A chill crawled up Megan's spine, and she hugged herself tightly. "It's just an old house," she whispered, her words swallowed by the eerie stillness. "Nothing to be afraid of."

But as she drew closer, the silence grew heavier, pressing against her eardrums. No crickets chirped, no leaves rustled. It was as if the very air held its breath in anticipation.

Megan's heart hammered against her ribs as she reached the crumbling steps. The porch boards creaked ominously under her weight. She hesitated, her hand hovering over the tarnished doorknob.

"I can do this," she thought, steeling herself. "It's just a Halloween party. Nothing more."

DEAD ENCOUNTER 89

With a deep breath, Megan pushed open the door. The hinges groaned, the sound reverberating through the foyer like a death rattle. She stepped inside, and her eyes widened in astonishment.

The interior was awash with flickering candlelight, illuminating a scene straight out of a history book. Dozens of people milled about in elaborate period costumes, their attire so authentic it made Megan's store-bought witch costume seem laughably out of place.

"Welcome, fair maiden," a young man in a powdered wig and brocade coat bowed deeply. "I trust your journey was not too taxing?"

Megan blinked, struggling to find her voice. "I... uh, no. It was fine."

She studied the man's costume, marveling at the intricate embroidery, the perfectly tailored fit. It didn't look like a costume at all, but like clothing he wore every day.

"This is incredible," Megan murmured, her earlier fear momentarily forgotten as curiosity took hold. "How did you get everything to look so real?"

The man tilted his head, confusion etching his features. "I'm afraid I don't understand your meaning, miss. These are simply my evening clothes."

A chill ran down Megan's spine. The man's archaic speech patterns, the utter conviction in his eyes – this was more than just dedicated roleplay. Something was very, very wrong.

"I need some air," Megan stammered, backing away. But as she turned, she found herself surrounded by a sea of unfamiliar faces, all dressed in styles spanning centuries. Their eyes bore into her, curious and hungry, as if she were the oddity in this gathering of ghosts.

Megan's heart raced as she forced a smile, her green eyes darting from face to face. "I'm Megan," she said, her voice wavering. "Megan Mathews. I'm new here."

A woman in a high-necked Victorian gown stepped forward, her blonde hair cascading down her back. "Meg-an?" she pronounced slowly, as if tasting an unfamiliar fruit. "What a peculiar name. I am Prudence Hawthorne."

"Jeremiah Hawthorne, at your service," the man in the brocade coat interjected with a flourish. "Though I confess, I've never heard the name Mathews in these parts."

Megan's brow furrowed. "But it's just a common last name. How could you not-"

"Abigail Thorne," a dark-haired woman in colonial attire cut in, her piercing blue eyes seeming to look through Megan rather than at her. "We welcome you to our... gathering."

Megan's fingers twisted nervously in the fabric of her costume. "Right. Nice to meet you all. This is quite the party."

As she mingled, snippets of conversation drifted to her ears, each more bewildering than the last.

"The harvest was bountiful this year, praise be," an elderly man in Puritan garb proclaimed.

"Did you hear? They're saying the telegraph might reach us by next autumn," a woman in a hoop skirt whispered excitedly.

Megan's mind reeled. These people weren't just in costume; they seemed to genuinely believe they were from different time periods. She caught Jeremiah's eye across the room, and he winked playfully.

This has to be some kind of elaborate prank, Megan thought desperately. *Maybe I've stumbled onto a historical reenactment society or something.*

But as she observed the effortless way they moved in their period clothing, the authentic accents and mannerisms, a chill crept up her spine.

Or maybe, a small voice in her head whispered, *this is something far stranger and more dangerous than you could have imagined.*

Megan's heart pounded as she ran her fingers over the intricately embroidered sleeve of a nearby party-goer. The fabric felt old, worn smooth by countless years of use. Her gaze darted from person to person, noticing the subtle differences in their attire - colonial ruffles here, Victorian lace there, even what looked like genuine flapper dresses from the 1920s.

"Oh God," she whispered, her breath catching in her throat. "These aren't costumes at all."

The realization hit her like a physical blow. These people, these teens, they weren't dressed up for a party. They were wearing the clothes they'd died in, centuries ago.

A hand touched her arm, making Megan jump. She whirled to find herself face to face with Abigail Thorne, the woman's piercing blue eyes boring into her.

"Thou seemest troubled, child," Abigail said, her voice soft yet carrying an undercurrent of ancient wisdom. "Pray, what vexes thee so?"

Megan swallowed hard, her mind racing. "I... I don't belong here," she managed to stammer out.

Abigail's lips curved into a enigmatic smile. "Dost thou not? And yet, here thou art, among us. Perhaps 'tis fate that hath guided thy steps to our humble gathering."

"Fate?" Megan echoed, her curiosity momentarily overriding her fear. "What do you mean?"

Abigail leaned closer, her words barely above a whisper. "The veil grows thin on All Hallows' Eve, child. The living and the dead, the past and the present - all become as one. But beware," she added, her grip on Megan's arm tightening, "for when the clock strikes twelve, the veil shall close once more."

Megan felt a chill run down her spine. *She knows,* she thought. *She knows they're all dead, and she knows I'm not. But why am I here? What's going to happen at midnight?*

As Megan's mind reeled from Abigail's cryptic warning, a jovial voice cut through her growing panic. "Ah, the belle of the ball! I've been simply dying to make your acquaintance."

Megan turned to find herself face-to-face with a dashing young man, his curly hair framing a mischievous grin. Jeremiah Hawthorne swept into an exaggerated bow, his 18th-century coat swirling around him.

"Jeremiah Hawthorne, at your service," he declared, taking Megan's hand and pressing a cool kiss to her knuckles. The touch sent shivers up her arm, a stark reminder of the unnatural nature of her surroundings.

"I... I'm Megan," she stammered, trying to regain her composure. "Megan Mathews."

Jeremiah's eyes twinkled with amusement. "A peculiar name for a peculiar night, wouldn't you agree?" He gestured around the room with a flourish. "Tell me, Miss Mathews, are you enjoying our little soirée?"

Megan's gaze darted nervously around the room, taking in the eerie, timeless faces of the other guests. "It's... certainly unique," she managed.

How do I tell him I know they're all dead? she wondered. *Or that I'm terrified I might join them?*

"Unique! Ha! What an delightfully understated way to put it," Jeremiah laughed, the sound both charming and unsettling. He leaned in close, his breath unnaturally cold against her ear. "But then, I suppose that's the appeal of our gathering. Where else can one dance with eternity?"

Before Megan could formulate a response, a quiet voice interjected. "Brother, you're frightening the poor girl."

A young woman in a flowing burgundy gown appeared at Jeremiah's side. Her long blonde hair framed a face of haunting beauty, marred only by the deep sadness in her eyes.

"Prudence, my dear sister!" Jeremiah exclaimed. "Come, let us make Miss Mathews feel welcome."

Prudence Hawthorne offered Megan a small, gentle smile. "Forgive my brother's exuberance," she said softly. "He forgets how... overwhelming our gatherings can be for newcomers."

Megan felt a flicker of warmth at Prudence's kind tone, a stark contrast to the chill permeating the air. "It's alright," she replied. "I'm just... trying to take it all in."

And figure out how to get out of here alive, she added silently.

Prudence's eyes seemed to see right through her. "It can be a lot to bear," she murmured. "The weight of so many lost souls, so many stories left unfinished." A shadow of pain crossed her face. "Sometimes I wonder if we're meant to find peace, or if we're doomed to relive this night for all eternity."

Jeremiah clapped his hands, breaking the somber mood. "Now, now, sister! Let's not dwell on such melancholy thoughts. The night is young, and there's merriment to be had!" He turned to Megan with a conspiratorial wink. "What say you, Miss Mathews? Shall we dance with death and see where the night takes us?"

Megan's heart raced as she glanced at the ornate grandfather clock looming in the corner. Its hands crept inexorably towards midnight, each tick echoing like a death knell in her ears. Panic clawed at her throat.

"I... I need some air," she stammered, backing away from Jeremiah and Prudence. Their eyes followed her, a mix of curiosity and something darker that made her skin crawl.

She stumbled through the crowd, the elaborate costumes now seeming to close in on her like a suffocating shroud. Megan's green eyes darted frantically, searching for an exit.

There has to be a way out, she thought desperately. *This can't be happening.*

"Leaving so soon, Miss Mathews?" Abigail's syrupy voice slithered from behind. "But the true revelry has yet to begin."

Megan whirled, her long brown hair whipping around her face. "I'm not feeling well," she lied, her voice trembling. "I should go."

Abigail's smile was a predator's grin. "Oh, but you can't leave now. You're part of us."

The grandfather clock began to chime, the sound reverberating through Megan's bones. One... Two...

"No!" Megan cried, shoving past Abigail. She ran, her heart hammering in time with the clock's relentless bongs.

Three... Four...

The mansion's layout seemed to shift and warp, corridors stretching endlessly. Megan's breath came in ragged gasps.

Five... Six...

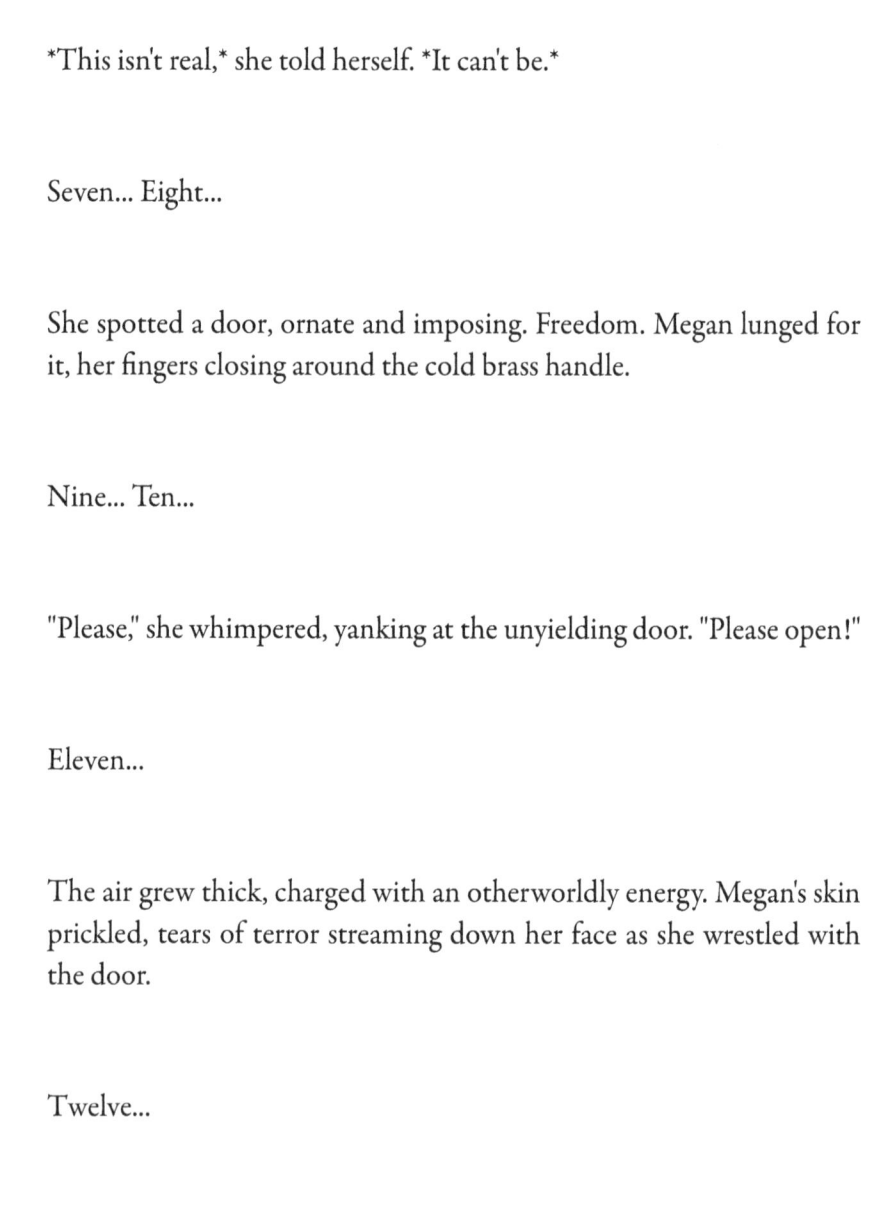

This isn't real, she told herself. *It can't be.*

Seven... Eight...

She spotted a door, ornate and imposing. Freedom. Megan lunged for it, her fingers closing around the cold brass handle.

Nine... Ten...

"Please," she whimpered, yanking at the unyielding door. "Please open!"

Eleven...

The air grew thick, charged with an otherworldly energy. Megan's skin prickled, tears of terror streaming down her face as she wrestled with the door.

Twelve...

As the final chime faded, a blinding flare of eldritch light erupted from every corner of the mansion. Megan screamed, the sound swallowed by the roar of otherworldly energy. The light was impossibly bright, searing her retinas and penetrating her very bones. It felt alive, hungry, consuming everything in its path.

In an instant, the world around her dissolved. The ornate door beneath her fingers vanished, leaving her grasping at empty air. The suffocating presence of the partygoers evaporated. Even the ground beneath her feet seemed to disappear.

When the light finally receded, Megan found herself standing alone on the empty plot where the mansion had stood moments before. The cool October air bit at her skin, a stark contrast to the stifling atmosphere inside. Her eyes, wide with disbelief, darted around frantically.

"No," she whispered, her voice hoarse. "No, no, no!"

Megan spun in a circle, her hair whipping around her face. There was no trace of the grand house, no sign of Abigail, Jeremiah, or any of the other guests. Only an overgrown lot remained, bathed in moonlight.

"This isn't possible," Megan muttered, her hands shaking as she hugged herself. "It was here. They were all here!"

But the empty night offered no answers, only an eerie silence that seemed to mock her confusion and fear.

Two years later, Megan sat hunched over her desk, surrounded by stacks of old newspapers and occult books. Her once vibrant green eyes were now shadowed by dark circles, her face gaunt with obsession. Pinned to the wall were maps of Willow Creek, covered in red strings and scribbled notes.

"I'm not crazy," she murmured, tracing a finger over a faded photograph of the mansion. "It happened. I know it happened."

A knock at her bedroom door made her jump. "Megan?" her mother's voice called. "Dinner's ready."

Megan sighed, running a hand through her tangled hair. "I'm not hungry, Mom," she called back.

"You need to eat, sweetie," her mother insisted, worry evident in her tone. "And maybe... maybe it's time to talk to someone again? Dr. Stevenson said-"

"I don't need another shrink!" Megan snapped, immediately regretting her harsh tone. She took a deep breath. "I'm fine, Mom. Really. I just... I need to figure this out."

As her mother's footsteps retreated, Megan turned back to her research, her fingers tracing the outlines of forgotten faces in the old photograph. "I'll prove it," she whispered to herself, a familiar determination settling over her. "I'll find out what really happened that night. No matter what it takes."

Megan's fingers trembled as she dialed Trevor's number, her heart pounding with a mix of hope and dread. The line crackled to life.

"Megs?" Trevor's voice was laced with concern. "It's been weeks. Are you okay?"

She swallowed hard, her throat constricting. "I found something, Trev. About the mansion."

A heavy sigh echoed through the receiver. "Megan, we've been through this-"

"No, listen!" Her words tumbled out in a frantic rush. "There's a historian in town, Thomas Sinclair. He's written about local legends, unexplained disappearances. I think he might believe me."

Silence stretched between them, thick with unspoken worry.

"Please," Megan whispered, her voice cracking. "Come with me. I need someone there who... who knew me before."

Trevor's hesitation was palpable. "Alright," he finally conceded. "But Megan, if this doesn't pan out-"

"It will," she insisted, ignoring the gnawing doubt in her gut. "It has to."

The next day, Megan stood before Thomas Sinclair's weathered Victorian home, Trevor at her side. The historian's study was a labyrinth of dusty tomes and arcane artifacts, the air heavy with the scent of old paper and secrets.

Thomas peered at them over wire-rimmed glasses, his eyes kind but shrewd. "So, Miss Mathews," he began, his
voice a soothing baritone. "Tell me about this... party."

As Megan recounted her tale, she felt the familiar tightness in her chest, the suffocating fear of that night. Trevor's skeptical glances burned into her, but Thomas listened intently, occasionally jotting notes in a leather-bound journal.

"Fascinating," Thomas murmured when she finished. He pulled a faded map from a nearby shelf. "The location you described... there are stories, whispers of a house that appears and vanishes. But never with such... specificity."

Hope bloomed in Megan's chest, fragile but fierce. "You believe me?"

Thomas's smile was gentle. "I believe there are more things in heaven and earth, Miss Mathews, than are dreamt of in our philosophy. Now," he leaned forward, eyes glinting with curiosity, "let's see what we can uncover together."

As they pored over ancient records, Megan felt a flicker of vindication. But beneath it all, a chilling thought persisted: what if uncovering the truth only led to greater horrors?

The autumnal twilight cast long shadows across Willow Creek's main street as Megan hurried towards the local bookshop, her heart pounding with a mixture of anticipation and dread. The bell above the door chimed ominously as she entered, the scent of old books and brewing tea enveloping her.

"Miss Mathews," a melodious voice called from the back of the store. "I've been expecting you."

Megan's breath caught in her throat as she laid eyes on Evelyn Blackwood for the first time. The woman's ageless beauty and piercing gaze sent a shiver down her spine.

"How did you know I was coming?" Megan asked, her voice wavering slightly.

Evelyn's lips curled into an enigmatic smile. "Some things are written in the stars, my dear. And some... in time itself."

Megan's mind raced. Could this woman truly know something about that fateful night?

"You seek answers about the Halloween party," Evelyn continued, her fingers tracing the spine of an ancient-looking tome. "But are you prepared for the truth?"

"I've been searching for two years," Megan replied, her determination evident in her clenched fists. "I need to know what happened."

Evelyn's eyes seemed to bore into her soul. "Knowledge comes at a price, Megan. The veil between worlds grows thin as All Hallows' Eve approaches. Are you willing to risk everything to lift it?"

A chill ran through Megan's body, but she stood her ground. "I can't keep living like this, not knowing. Whatever the cost, I'll pay it."

"Very well," Evelyn whispered, her voice carrying an otherworldly resonance. She pulled a small, ornate key from her pocket. "When the time comes, you'll know how to use this. But remember, once you step through that door, there's no turning back."

As Megan's trembling fingers closed around the key, the shop seemed to darken, shadows stretching impossibly long. For a moment, she thought she glimpsed figures moving in the gloom – familiar faces from that haunting night.

"Until we meet again, Megan Mathews," Evelyn's voice echoed as she seemingly melted into the shadows. "May the fates be kind."

Clutching the key to her chest, Megan stumbled out of the shop. The crisp October air did little to calm her racing thoughts. Halloween was less than a week away. Whatever answers awaited her, whatever horrors she might face, she knew she had to see this through.

"I'm coming back," she whispered to the gathering darkness. "And this time, I'll uncover the truth – no matter what."

THE GHOST CHILD

Lucas Everhart's sneakers crunched against the gravel as he approached the forsaken threshold of Willow Creek's most whispered-about relic. A gentle breeze toyed with the hem of his jacket, carrying whispers from the past as if the mansion itself had been waiting for him.

"Here goes nothing," he murmured to himself, pushing open the creaking door that protested with a groan. The boy's heart hammered in his chest, echoing through the silence like a drumbeat calling him forth.

Curiosity flickered in his bright green eyes, scanning the foyer where dust danced in the slivers of light piercing through boarded-up windows. Each step stirred the settled history beneath his feet, and cobwebs clung to his sweater as tangible reminders of the mansion's long abandonment.

"Kinda creepy... I love it," Lucas whispered with a half-grin, wiping away the webs with a determined sweep of his hand.

The wood underfoot groaned as if in response to his presence, and Lucas took a tentative step toward the grand staircase, its once-opulent rails now blanketed in decay. With each careful ascent, the weight of countless untold stories seemed to press upon his shoulders.

"Come find me..." The faint whisper was barely audible, a siren song woven into the stillness. Lucas paused, head tilting, listening. He wasn't alone.

"Hello?" His voice was louder than he intended, an invasion on the silent sanctum. The whispers morphed into a hushed giggle, a sound both chilling and compelling. "Who's there?"

He reached the landing, greeted by a gloomy corridor lined with doors that held secrets in their silence. The whispers beckoned him forward, a ghostly hand guiding him deeper into the mansion's embrace.

"Guess we're playing hide and seek, huh?" Lucas muttered, his adventurous spirit undeterred by the eerie game unfolding.

His eyes adjusted to the dimness, catching sight of faded wallpaper peeling like aged skin from the walls. Each step felt calculated, the anticipation building as he neared the bedroom at the hallway's end.

"Alright, I'll bite. Let's see what you're hiding," he said, steeling himself with a gulp as he laid a hand on the door handle, cold to the touch. The whispers crescendoed into a hushed crescendo, urging him to unveil the room's secrets.

With a deep breath, Lucas twisted the knob and pushed, the door swinging open to reveal the chamber where the past lingered, ever-present, and waiting for him.

Lucas's breath caught in his throat as the room materialized before him. Moonlight spilled through a crack in the curtains, casting a spectral glow over the dusty chamber. His eyes darted around, scanning the antique furniture and the faded portraits that observed in silence until they landed on a figure by the window.

"Thomas?" Lucas's voice was barely a whisper, disbelief lacing each syllable.

The figure turned, and Lucas's heart sank. Thomas Holloway stood before him, his skin an unnatural shade of white, his eyes hollow pools reflecting a tormented soul. Lucas stumbled back, the sight of his once vibrant friend now reduced to a ghostly apparition sending shivers down his spine.

"Lucas," Thomas spoke, his voice a mere echo of itself, "you have to help me."

"Thomas, what happened to you?" Lucas's fear was quickly replaced by resolve as he stepped forward, determined to aid his friend.

"An ancient curse... it binds me here," Thomas murmured, his gaze fixed on Lucas with a silent plea.

"Then we'll break it," Lucas declared, the weight of his promise hanging heavy in the air. He looked into Thomas's eyes, the unwavering loyalty to his friend fueling his courage.

Leaving the mansion with a purpose, Lucas made haste to the town's library, where he knew Edith Moore would still be poring over her books, a guardian of knowledge in the quiet hours. The bell above the library door tinkled as he entered, the familiar scent of old paper greeting him.

"Edith!" Lucas called out, urgency sharpening his tone.

"Lucas Everhart," Edith greeted, peering over her glasses with a mix of surprise and curiosity. "What brings you here so late?"

"It's Thomas. I found him in the mansion," Lucas began, his words tumbling out in a rush.

"Take a breath, child," Edith said softly, closing the book she was reading. "Start from the beginning."

Lucas recounted his eerie encounter, watching as Edith's expression turned somber. She rose from her chair, moving to a section of the library that Lucas had never seen her navigate before.

"An ancient curse, you say?" Edith murmured, scanning the spines of musty tomes. "I've read stories about such things binding spirits to places of great sorrow."

"Can it be broken?" Lucas asked, hope threading through his desperation.

"Perhaps," Edith said, pulling down a thick volume bound in leather. "There are ways, rituals of old, but they are not to be taken lightly."

"Tell me what to do," Lucas insisted, his determination burning bright.

"Very well," Edith relented, opening the book to a page marked by a folded corner. "But you must prepare yourself, Lucas. What lies ahead is fraught with peril."

"Whatever it takes," Lucas affirmed, leaning in to examine the faded text. "For Thomas."

Together, they pored over the ancient script, Edith guiding him through the arcane words while outside, the night deepened, holding its breath for the trials to come.

Lucas's footsteps crunched on the gravel path as he approached Clara's house, his heart thumping against his ribcage like a frantic drum. The sun had begun its descent, casting long shadows across the yard where Clara was tending to a wounded rabbit, her gentle hands working deftly with a bandage.

"Clara," Lucas called out, his voice betraying an urgency that made her look up from her task, brown eyes reflecting concern.

"Lucas? What's wrong?" she asked, standing and brushing her hands on her jeans.

"Thomas... I spoke with Miss Edith," he began, breathless. "There's a way to help him."

The words hung in the air for a moment as Clara's eyes widened. "How?"

"An ancient ritual. But it's dangerous," Lucas admitted, his gaze holding hers. "I can't do this alone."

"Take me there," Clara said without hesitation, her resolve hardening. "I'll do anything to save my brother."

Together, they made their way to the mansion, the grand structure looming ominously against the darkening sky. With each step, the air grew colder, the silence around them deeper.

"Remember, Thomas might not be... himself," Lucas warned as they crossed the threshold into the dusty foyer, their presence disturbing the cobwebs that festooned the chandelier overhead.

"Lucas! Clara!" The ghostly voice echoed from upstairs, a whisper of desperation.

"Thomas!" Clara cried out, racing ahead with Lucas at her heels. They found Thomas in the same bedroom, his spectral form flickering like a candle in the wind.

"Thomas, we're going to help you," Clara said, reaching out to touch his hand, her fingers slipping through his ethereal skin.

"Careful," Lucas murmured. "The curse..."

"Look at this," Thomas interrupted, pointing to a faded painting on the wall. It depicted the original owners of the mansion, their figures stern and foreboding. "She knows."

"Who?" Clara asked, following his gaze.

"Cecilia Blackwood," Thomas replied. "The last of them. She holds the key."

Lucas stepped closer to the painting, his eyes scanning the details. "We need to find her, talk to her."

"Will she help us?" Clara wondered aloud, her voice tinged with uncertainty.

"We have to try," Lucas said resolutely. "For your sake, Thomas, we will confront the past."

They turned back to the dimly lit hallway, their shadows stretching behind them as they ventured deeper into the mansion. Each room whispered secrets, the legacy of sorrow etched into the very walls.

"Promise me," Thomas said, his voice barely above a whisper. "Promise me freedom."

"Promise," Lucas and Clara said together, their voices a chorus of hope in the haunted silence. They left the mansion that evening, the weight of destiny heavy upon their shoulders, determined to unlock the history that held their friend captive.

Lucas's hand hovered over the ornate brass knocker, his heart thudding against his ribs. With a glance at Clara, who nodded her encouragement, he rapped sharply on Cecilia Blackwood's heavy wooden door. It swung open with an eerie creak, revealing the silver-haired woman standing as if she had been expecting them.

"Lucas Everhart, Clara Milton," Cecilia greeted, her voice the whisper of silk. "I presume you've come for answers."

"About the mansion," Lucas said, stepping into the dimly lit foyer. "And about Thomas."

"Your friend is lost to a curse my family has long borne," she replied, leading them through the labyrinthine corridors of her home. The air was thick with the scent of must and old paper.

"Your brother, Elijah," Clara began hesitantly, "he's part of all this, isn't he?"

Cecilia halted, her eyes flickering like storm clouds. "Elijah has always dabbled in matters beyond our ken. His betrayal runs deep, deeper than the roots of Willow Creek."

"What has he done?" Lucas asked, the weight of dread settling in his stomach.

"Used the curse for himself," Cecilia confessed, her words laced with sorrow. "To sustain his own life, forever caught between time's relentless march and the stillness of death."

"Immortality," Clara whispered, horror-struck.

"Indeed," Cecilia affirmed. "But such power comes at a price. Souls are the currency he trades in."

"Thomas..." Lucas's fists clenched.

"Is but one of many," she finished gravely.

Suddenly, the house shuddered, as if in agreement, and a cold wind whipped through the halls. Lucas exchanged a glance with Clara; they both knew time was slipping away like sand through their fingers.

"We need to break the curse," declared Lucas, his resolve hardening.

"Before more lives are lost," added Clara, her voice steady despite the fear that shone in her eyes.

"Then you must act swiftly," Cecilia advised. "The mansion grows hungry, its appetite insatiable. With each passing moment, the supernatural forces within gain strength."

"Tell us how to stop it," Lucas demanded.

"Knowledge rests within the mansion," she said cryptically. "Seek the heart of the house, where shadows dance and time weeps. Only there will you find your salvation."

"Let's go," Clara urged, gripping Lucas's arm. "We don't have much time."

"Be wary," Cecilia called out as they hastened back toward the mansion. "Elijah will not let his secret die easily."

"Neither will we," Lucas called back, thoughts racing as fast as his pulse. They sprinted across the grounds, the ghostly pallor of the mansion rising before them like an omen.

"Thomas!" Clara shouted as they burst through the doors. "We know about Elijah!"

"Quickly," Thomas's spectral form drifted toward them, urgency flickering in his hollow eyes. "The heart of the house—it's changing. Becoming stronger."

"Lead the way," Lucas said, determination etching his features.

Together, they plunged into the depths of the mansion, every echo a reminder of the ticking clock, every shadow a testament to the danger that lay ahead.

Lucas's fingers trembled as they traced the ornate symbols etched into the leather-bound cover of the ancient text. The dim light from his flashlight danced across the pages, revealing a language that twisted and turned like the roots of an old tree.

"Look at this," he whispered to Clara, who peered over his shoulder, her breath forming a ghostly mist in the chill air of the library.

"Can you read it?" she asked, her voice low and tense.

"Some of it," Lucas replied, his eyes narrowing in concentration. "It's a ritual... We need the moon, Clara. The full moon, and it's... It's only three days away."

"Three days?" Clara echoed, her freckles lost in the pallor of concern that washed over her face. "That's not enough time."

"We have to make it enough." Lucas snapped the book closed, resolve hardening in his bright green eyes.

"Guys," Thomas's ethereal voice cut through the silence, a note of urgency threading his words. "There's more to worry about than just time."

Lucas and Clara spun around to see the translucent figure of their friend pointing towards the window. Sheriff Thompson stood outside, flashlight in hand, its beam slicing through the darkness as he scanned the mansion's perimeter.

"Damn," Lucas muttered. "He's getting too close."

"Let's move to the attic," Clara suggested, her chestnut hair swaying as she grabbed the ancient text from Lucas's grasp. "He won't find us there."

The three of them hurried up the creaking staircase, the musty scent of decay growing stronger with every step. They settled amongst trunks of forgotten memories and cobwebs that veiled the past like gossamer curtains.

"Okay," Clara breathed out, opening the book once again. "We'll study this here. But we need to be careful. If Sheriff Thompson catches us—"

"Then we're done for," Lucas finished for her, his tousled brown hair falling into his eyes as he leaned closer to examine the text. "But we can't let that happen. We have to free Thomas and stop Elijah."

"Agreed," Thomas said, his spectral form hovering anxiously beside them. "I don't want anyone else trapped because of me."

"Alright, then." Lucas ran his hands through his hair, setting his jaw firmly. "We'll take shifts keeping watch. Clara, you start deciphering the text with me. Thomas, you alert us if anything changes outside."

"Got it," Clara nodded, pulling her sweater tighter around her as she focused on the ancient writings.

"Be careful," Thomas warned, drifting towards the window where the moonlight cast his outline in a melancholy glow. "Elijah isn't our only threat now."

As they poured over the cryptic instructions, whispers of the past seemed to bleed from the pages, mingling with the urgency of the present. Lucas felt the weight of their task settle upon him, a mantle of responsibility that he was determined to carry to the end. With each word they decoded, the path forward became clearer, and the stakes climbed ever higher.

Lucas's fingers traced the delicate script of the ancient text, his brow furrowed in concentration. Beside him, Clara leaned closer, her breath quick and quiet as she deciphered the archaic language aloud. The air in the dusty library was thick with anticipation, the only light coming from the flickering candles casting long shadows across their faces.

"Here, this part," Clara pointed to a line etched with symbols that seemed to dance before Lucas's eyes. "It speaks of the balance between light and dark, life and death."

"Balance...yes, I think I've got it!" Lucas exclaimed, feeling a surge of excitement. Their preparation had been meticulous, every step toward freeing Thomas measured and deliberate. But as the moon outside crept toward its zenith, an ominous chill seeped through the room, causing the candle flames to shiver.

Without warning, the heavy door burst open with a resounding crash, sending a gust of wind that snuffed out the candles. In the doorway loomed Elijah Blackwood, his antiquated clothing rippling around him like the darkness itself.

"Your efforts are admirable but futile," he intoned, his voice echoing with haunting resonance. "You cannot hope to understand the forces you meddle with."

"Stay back, Elijah!" Clara shouted, her voice quivering with a mix of fear and defiance. Lucas stood protectively in front of her, clutching the text to his chest.

"Give me the book, boy," Elijah demanded, advancing with measured steps, the floorboards creaking under his weight. "You have no idea what you're dealing with."

"Over my dead body," Lucas spat, determination hardening his young features.

With a swift motion, Elijah's hand shot out, wresting the text from Lucas's grasp. Pages fluttered to the ground like wounded birds as he tore the book apart, pieces of ancient knowledge scattering into oblivion. Clara screamed, her sound of despair mingling with the howl of the wind outside.

"NO!" Lucas lunged forward, but it was too late; the remnants of the text lay in ruins at Elijah's feet.

"Thomas is mine," Elijah said coldly. "Forever bound to this place."

As Elijah vanished as quickly as he'd appeared, leaving behind a void where hope once flickered, Lucas dropped to his knees among the remnants of the pages, his heart sinking into desolation.

"Lucas, we can't give up," Clara said, her voice hoarse as she knelt beside him, placing a trembling hand on his shoulder.

"It's over, Clara. Without the text..." Lucas's words trailed off, the enormity of their loss settling heavily upon them.

Then, like a beacon piercing the darkness, Edith Moore's voice called out from the doorway, her figure silhouetted by the hallway's dim light. "Not all is lost, children."

"Ms. Moore?" Lucas looked up, hope flickering in his green eyes.

"Quickly, come with me." Edith beckoned them urgently. "There's something you need to see."

In her library sanctuary, surrounded by the scent of old books and wisdom, Edith produced a carefully wrapped bundle from a locked drawer. Unfolding the cloth, she revealed an exact copy of the text.

"I feared something like this might happen," Edith explained, her half-moon glasses glinting. "So I took the liberty of making a duplicate, just in case."

"Edith, you're brilliant!" Clara exclaimed, her relief palpable.

"Thank you," Lucas breathed, his resolve reigniting. "But how do we confront Elijah now? He's more powerful than we imagined."

"Knowledge is power, Lucas," Edith reminded them, her eyes shining with a wisdom born of countless tales both lived and read. "And together, we have enough to turn the tide."

"Let's plan," Clara said, her soft voice now imbued with newfound strength.

Together, they poured over the copied text, piecing together a strategy not just of rituals and incantations, but of courage and unity. Elijah Blackwood had destroyed a book, but he hadn't shattered their spirit. With Edith's copy, they held the key to breaking the curse that bound their friend and confronting the darkness with the light of hope.

"Lucas, now!" Clara's voice cut through the howling wind as lightning fractured the sky above the forsaken mansion. They stood in the ritual circle, the copied text clutched tightly in Lucas's hands.

"By the ancient powers," Lucas recited, his voice a steady anchor amidst the chaos, "we break the chains of time and spirit."

Elijah Blackwood emerged from the shadows, his figure almost ethereal against the backdrop of the storm. "Fools," he sneered, his eyes dark pools of malice. "You think you can defy the curse that has given me eternity?"

"Thomas doesn't belong to you!" Clara shouted back, her expression resolute despite the fear that trembled in her words.

"Nor does this town," Thomas added quietly, his spectral form shimmering with an inner light that seemed to push against the surrounding darkness.

"Your time is over, Elijah!" Lucas called out, turning the pages of the text with fingers numb from the cold. The air was electric with the power of the impending incantation.

"Lucas, the salt!" Clara reminded him, her own hand throwing a handful into the wind. The granules twisted in the air, forming a protective barrier around them.

"Ex spiritus liberate!" Lucas continued, his green eyes blazing with defiance as the winds whipped his hair wildly around his face.

Elijah advanced, his form blurring like a mirage, but the salt held him at bay. "I will not be undone by children!" His voice was a thunderous roar, but it wavered, betraying a hint of desperation.

"Lucas, the final words!" Thomas urged, his voice clear and strong despite the tumult.

"Corpus, mente, et anima!" Lucas felt the energy of the ritual peak, a crescendo of hope and determination focusing through him.

"Finish it!" Clara cried out, clutching Thomas's ethereal hand, anchoring her brother with all her might.

"Redime!" Lucas exclaimed, and a brilliant burst of light exploded from the center of the circle, engulfing everything.

The storm raged on for a moment longer before it began to dissipate as quickly as it had arrived, the supernatural tempest quelled by the power of the ritual. The mansion groaned and creaked, as if waking from a long slumber, its sinister presence retreating with each passing second.

Elijah Blackwood's form wavered, contorted in an expression of anguish and defeat before vanishing into the ether, his immortality finally succumbing to the relentless march of time.

As calm settled, Lucas, Clara, and Thomas remained within the circle, their breaths visible in the chilled silence. Thomas's gaze met Lucas's, gratitude and relief evident in his piercing blue eyes.

"Thank you," Thomas whispered, his voice like a melody fading into the stillness. And then, with a gentle smile, he stepped forward and dissolved into the air, his spirit finally freed from the accursed mansion.

"Thomas," Clara murmured, tears mingling with raindrops on her cheeks. Yet there was peace in her sorrow, a knowing that her brother was now where he belonged—beyond the veil, released from his earthly bonds.

Lucas looked around at the quiet mansion, feeling the weight of what they had accomplished settle around him. They had faced the darkness, together, and emerged victorious. The curse was broken; their friend was free. And Willow Creek, once overshadowed by the haunting specter of the past, could now look toward a brighter future.

The morning sun stretched its golden fingers through the tattered curtains of the once-oppressive mansion, casting a gentle glow over the foyer where Lucas stood. He glanced at Clara, noting the resolve etched in her features as Cecilia Blackwood took a deliberate step forward, her silver hair glinting with the light of dawn.

"It's time to mend what has been broken," Cecilia said, her voice resonating with a newfound purpose. She turned her haunting gray eyes upon them, and for the first time, Lucas saw the burden of centuries fall away from her shoulders.

"Thank you, Cecilia," Clara replied, her voice soft yet firm. "For honoring Thomas's memory by facing your family's past."

Cecilia nodded solemnly, her gaze lingering on the spot where Thomas had vanished. "He was the light that guided us out of darkness. I shall not let his sacrifice be in vain."

Lucas swallowed hard against the lump in his throat. "We should go, Clara. Let the house rest, just like Thomas."

Clara nodded, and together they stepped out of the mansion, leaving its doors ajar—like an invitation to lay old ghosts to rest.

They walked in silence through the streets of Willow Creek, the town stirring to life around them. Children laughed on their way to school, unaware of the monumental shift that had occurred while they slept.

"Lucas," Clara said, breaking the quiet, "do you think we'll ever see Thomas again?"

"Maybe," Lucas replied, his green eyes reflecting the hope that bloomed in his heart. "In our dreams, or on the edge of twilight when the world is full of mysteries."

Clara smiled, a wistful expression playing across her face. "I'd like that."

At the edge of town, where the concrete gave way to dirt paths and wildflowers, they paused. Lucas looked back at the receding silhouette of the mansion, now just a part of the landscape.

"Go on, Clara. I want to remember this place, just for a moment more."

She squeezed his hand and continued down the path, leaving Lucas alone with his thoughts.

He closed his eyes, breathing in the earthy scent of the forest that bordered Willow Creek. When he opened them again, he saw his town with new eyes—a place of hidden depths and boundless wonder.

"Goodbye, Thomas," he whispered to the wind, imagining his friend's spirit soaring high above the trees, finally free.

Turning his back on the mansion, Lucas made his way home. His sneakers scuffed familiar pavement, each step a reminder of the adventures he had lived and the bonds he had forged.

"Hey, Lucas!" Mrs. Jenkins called out from her porch as he passed by, her tabby cat winding around her ankles. "You look like you've seen a ghost!"

"Something like that, Mrs. Jenkins," Lucas replied with a grin, feeling the truth of his own words less like a weight and more like a badge of honor.

"Be careful out there," she advised, her eyes twinkling with unspoken understanding.

"I will," Lucas promised, knowing that mystery would always be a part of him, just as much as the blood running through his veins and the memories etched into his soul.

As he reached the modest Everhart residence, Lucas took a deep breath before opening the front door. The familiar smells of breakfast wafted out to him, and he could hear his mother humming a tune in the kitchen.

"Lucas, is that you?" his mother called out.

"Yep, it's me, Mom!" Lucas responded, stepping inside.

He hung up his backpack, the trusty companion of many adventures, and felt the normalcy of his life wrap around him like a warm embrace.

"Have a good walk?" his mother asked, peering at him with a curious smile as he entered the kitchen.

"More than good, Mom," Lucas said, his heart swelling with the secret knowledge of all that he and his friends had achieved. "It was... enlightening."

"Sounds mysterious," she teased, placing a plate of pancakes in front of him.

"Maybe I'll tell you about it someday," Lucas said, taking a bite and tasting the sweetness of victory.

As he ate, his mind wandered to the mansion, to Thomas, to Clara, and to the unbreakable threads that connected them all. Lucas Everhart, the curious boy with the bright green eyes, had returned home, but he knew he would never be the same.

After all, some mysteries don't just change what you know—they change who you are.

Lucas's sneakers crunched on the gravel as he raced along the sun-dappled path that led to their next potential adventure. Clara's breathless laughter trailed behind him as they burst through the underbrush, the thrill of discovery urging them onward.

"Slow down, Lucas!" Clara called out, her voice laced with mirth and mock frustration.

He glanced over his shoulder, grinning at her flushed face. "Come on, we're almost there!"

They came to a halt at the edge of Willow Creek's infamous lake, its surface eerily still, reflecting the somber gray clouds overhead like a dark mirror. The air around them felt heavy, charged with an unspoken warning that tightened Lucas's chest with anticipation.

"Wow," Clara whispered beside him, her brown eyes wide as she took in the view. "It's... unsettling."

"Remember what Old Man Harris said? About the lake claiming lives?" Lucas's words tumbled out with fervent curiosity.

"Hard to forget a tale like that," Clara replied, inching closer to the water's edge, her usual caution giving way to intrigue.

"Look there!" Lucas pointed to a half-submerged rowboat swaying gently in the middle of the lake. "It's like it's been abandoned right where..."

"Where the last disappearance happened." Clara finished his sentence, her voice barely above a whisper.

A sudden gust of wind whipped across the lake, sending shivers down Lucas's spine. He watched as the ripples disrupted the reflection, distorting the once calm waters into a chaotic dance.

"Lucas, do you feel that?" Clara asked, hugging herself as another chill coursed through the air.

"Like we're not alone?" His hand instinctively reached for the flashlight in his backpack even though daylight surrounded them.

"Exactly." Clara nodded, her gaze fixed on the murky depths. "There are stories about this place, whispers of something beneath the water, something that doesn't rest."

"Then let's find out what it is," Lucas declared, his tone resolute. This was what they did—uncover the hidden, shed light on the shadows. It was more than just a pastime; it was a calling.

"Okay, but we need to be careful," Clara cautioned, always the voice of reason to his impulsive nature. "Whatever is here, it's not friendly."

"Agreed. We'll start by checking around the shore, look for clues." Lucas stepped back from the water's edge, suddenly aware of the danger lurking beneath the placid surface.

"Maybe we can find out what happened to those who disappeared," Clara suggested, falling into step beside him as they began their cautious investigation.

"Or maybe we'll find out why they never came back," Lucas added, his heart pounding with a mixture of fear and excitement.

Together, they walked the perimeter of the haunted lake, their senses heightened, ready to delve into the new mystery that Willow Creek had offered up. For Lucas and Clara, every whisper of the unknown was an invitation, and every shadow held a story waiting to be told.

Lucas rapped on the door of the Willow Creek Public Library with a sense of urgency that matched the quickening beat of his heart. Beside him, Clara fidgeted nervously, her eyes scanning the dim street as the evening crept in like a silent specter.

"Edith will know what to do," Lucas whispered, more to himself than to reassure Clara.

The door creaked open, and there stood Edith Moore, her familiar half-moon glasses reflecting the dying light. "Back again so soon?" she inquired, though the twinkle in her eye betrayed her delight at their visit.

"Ms. Moore, we need your help," Clara said, her voice steady despite the chill that had nothing to do with the temperature.

"Come in, come in," Edith beckoned them inside the library, a sanctuary of knowledge amidst a town teeming with secrets.

Once seated at a sturdy oak table laden with ancient texts and local history volumes, Lucas wasted no time. "It's the lake this time," he said, his gaze locked onto Edith's. "People have gone missing, and we think... we think it's haunted."

"Haunted?" Edith echoed, her brow furrowing as she adjusted her glasses. "Tell me everything you've seen and heard."

As Lucas and Clara recounted their observations and the eerie tales whispered by the townsfolk, Edith listened intently, her fingers occasionally brushing against the spines of nearby books as if they were old friends sharing their wisdom.

"Let's see," Edith murmured, standing and moving toward a section of shelves that groaned under the weight of their literary burden. She pulled out a hefty volume bound in leather that looked as though it hadn't been touched in ages. Dust motes danced in the beam of light filtering through a nearby window as she laid the book before them.

"This is the collected history of Willow Creek," Edith explained, flipping through pages until she stopped at a chapter marked with a small, faded ribbon. "Ah, here it is—the story of Lake Whispers."

"Whispers?" Clara leaned forward, her curiosity piqued.

"Indeed," Edith confirmed, her finger tracing the lines of text. "Many years ago, a family lived by the lake. The Whitmans. They were happy until tragedy struck—their youngest daughter drowned under mysterious circumstances. Heartbroken, they say her mother couldn't bear the loss. She walked into the lake one night, never to return."

"Restless spirits," Lucas muttered, piecing together the sorrow-filled tale with the disappearances.

"Legend has it," Edith continued, her voice low as if carrying the weight of the story, "that the mother's spirit still searches for her daughter, calling out to the living, drawing them into the depths in her grief."

"Could that be why people are vanishing now?" Clara asked, a shiver running down her spine.

"Possibly," Edith conceded. "If the spirits are indeed restless, they may be reaching out, ensnaring those who wander too close to the water's edge."

"Then we need to find a way to put them to rest," Lucas stated, determination setting his jaw firm. "For the Whitmans and for Willow Creek."

"Be cautious, children," Edith warned. "Such things are not easily settled, and the line between the living and the dead can become perilously thin."

"Thank you, Ms. Moore," Clara said, gratitude mingling with resolve in her soft voice.

"Of course," Edith replied, offering them a brave smile. "And remember, knowledge is light in the darkness. Use it wisely."

Armed with the tragic history of Lake Whispers, Lucas and Clara left the library, their minds alight with thoughts of spirits trapped in perpetual sorrow and a community in need of protection. Together, they set out into the enveloping night, ready to face the shadows cast upon the waters of Willow Creek.

Lucas squatted at the edge of Lake Whispers, his reflection a distorted echo on the shimmering surface. "The water's so still, it's like glass," he murmured, watching a lone leaf drift by.

"Too still," Clara whispered beside him, clutching her backpack straps tight. "It's like the lake is holding its breath."

"Edith said the mother's spirit is looking for her daughter, right?" Lucas glanced up, meeting Clara's somber eyes. "What if we give them a way to find each other?"

"Like a beacon?" Clara's brow furrowed in thought.

"Exactly!" Lucas's voice held an edge of excitement. "We could use light—lanterns on the water. They could symbolize guidance, hope."

Clara nodded slowly, her face brightening. "And candles," she added. "To represent the souls of Mrs. Whitman and her daughter."

"Let's do it tonight," Lucas decided, standing up and brushing off his hands. "We'll need to be quick though, before anyone else gets too close."

"Okay, but we have to be careful," Clara cautioned, her voice a ghostly whisper against the hush of twilight.

"Always are," Lucas assured her with a grin that belied the gravity of their task.

Night cloaked the lake as they returned, armed with lanterns and candles. Lucas lit a match, the flare briefly illuminating his determined gaze before he touched it to a candlewick.

"Mrs. Whitman," Clara spoke softly into the darkness, "we're here to help you find peace."

One by one, they set the lanterns and candles onto the placid surface. The soft glow danced across the water, creating a path of flickering light.

"Look, it's working!" Lucas exclaimed as a gentle breeze stirred, nudging the lanterns forward.

But the calm was short-lived. A chill descended, creeping along their spines as the water began to ripple, the reflections distorting into elongated shapes. A mournful wail rose from the depths, sending ripples through the night air.

"Lucas, the spirits are restless," Clara said, her voice trembling but resolute.

"Stay close," he replied, grabbing her hand.

Shapes emerged from the water, ethereal and sorrowful, their cries mingling with the wind. Lucas and Clara stood firm, their eyes fixed on the spectral figures.

"It's okay," Clara called out, projecting warmth into her quivering tone. "Your family is waiting for you. Follow the lights."

The howls softened, turning to whispers as the spirits drew nearer to the lanterns. The shadowy figures of a woman and a child became discernible, reaching out to each other amidst the glow.

"Keep talking, Clara. It's helping," Lucas urged, squeezing her hand for courage.

"Find each other," Clara continued, her voice now a soothing lullaby. "Let the light guide you home."

A hushed peace settled over the lake as the spirits united, the light from the lanterns enveloping them in a serene embrace. Slowly, the apparitions faded, the echoes of their departure lingering like a final sigh.

Lucas and Clara watched, breathless, as the last wisps of mist dissolved, and the lake returned to its undisturbed state.

"We did it," Lucas exhaled, the weight of the night lifting from his shoulders.

"Thanks to you," Clara said, a small, relieved smile touching her lips.

"Thanks to us," Lucas corrected gently, knowing they had faced the unknown together—and triumphed.

The gentle waves of Willow Creek's haunted lake now lapped quietly against the shore, a stark contrast to the turmoil that had so recently raged. Lucas turned to Clara, his green eyes mirroring her relief.

"Looks like the stories will have to change," he said softly. "No more hauntings at this lake."

Clara, standing shoulder to shoulder with him, smiled and nodded, her chestnut hair catching the glint of the morning sun. "Just tales of two friends who wouldn't give up on the past—or each other."

Together, they walked back into town, the weight of their backpacks somehow feeling lighter. It wasn't long before word spread of their daring night by the lake. Shopkeepers stepped out onto the sidewalks, hats in hand, nodding with respect as the pair passed. Children ran alongside them, peppering them with questions, eyes wide with wonder.

"Lucas! Clara! Did you really talk to the ghosts?" one bold youngster asked, his voice tinged with awe.

"Maybe we just listened," Lucas replied with a wink, nudging Clara playfully.

At the center of town, Mayor Henley awaited them, his face etched with gratitude. "Lucas, Clara, you've done something extraordinary," he declared, his voice carrying across the gathering crowd. "You've freed our town from fear, returned peace to troubled souls, and reminded us all of the power of compassion."

A cheer erupted from the townsfolk, a ripple of applause washing over the square. Clara blushed, unaccustomed to such attention, but Lucas stood tall, pride swelling in his chest.

"Thank you, Mr. Mayor," Clara said, her soft voice steady now. "But we couldn't have done it without everyone's support—and the memories of those who were lost."

"Indeed." The mayor nodded solemnly before breaking into a broad smile. "Let's celebrate these brave young heroes!"

Music filled the air as an impromptu festival sprang to life. Tables laden with food lined the streets, and laughter replaced the whispers of superstition. Lucas and Clara were hoisted onto shoulders and paraded around like champions of old, their faces beaming in the sunlight.

"Lucas," Clara murmured as the festivities swirled around them, "do you think Thomas would be proud?"

"Without a doubt," Lucas assured her, squeezing her hand. "He's with us, Clara. Today, we celebrate for him, too."

As the sun began to set, painting the sky in hues of orange and purple, the celebration continued. Stories were shared, futures were toasted, and two friends stood at the heart of it all, their bond unbreakable, their hearts full.

In the warmth of the fading day, the fears that had once shrouded Willow Creek dissolved, and hope—like the lanterns they'd used to guide the spirits—shone brightly, leading the way forward.

The twilight held a gentle hush over Willow Creek as Lucas Everhart padded down the creaky steps of his front porch, the remnants of celebration still clinging to his skin like the faintest summer sweat. The echo of laughter had long since vanished into the night, and the stars peered curiously down upon him, silent witnesses to the quiet respite that had settled upon the town.

"Lucas!" Clara's voice sliced through the calm, her silhouette framed by the glow of the streetlamp as she hurried toward him, an envelope clutched in her hand. "Look what I found on your doorstep."

"Another thank-you note?" Lucas asked, taking the envelope. His fingers traced the heavy paper, unusually thick and sealed with red wax—a stark contrast to the celebratory cards they'd been receiving.

"Doesn't seem like it," Clara replied, peering over his shoulder as Lucas carefully broke the seal and unfolded the letter inside.

Dear Mr. Everhart,

As the whispers of the past settle, let this serve as a harbinger of what is yet to come. The victory you cherish is but a prelude to a storm that looms on the horizon. Brace yourself, for the shadows grow hungry once again.

"Who would send something like this?" Clara's voice quivered slightly with unease, her earlier bravery giving way to the creeping tendrils of fear.

"Someone who knows too much—or thinks they do," Lucas murmured, rereading the cryptic warning. His heart, still buoyant from their recent success, began to sink with the weight of impending dread.

"Lucas, we've dealt with worse," Clara said, though her attempt at reassurance did little to dispel the chill that had begun to seep into the evening air. "Let's not jump to conclusions until we've figured out where this came from."

"Right." Lucas nodded, his mind churning with possibilities as he folded the letter and tucked it back into its envelope. His green eyes, usually alight with curiosity, now bore a determined glint. "We start first thing tomorrow."

"Agreed," Clara said, a newfound resolve setting her jaw firm. "This town has seen enough darkness. We won't let it fall under another shadow."

"Come on," Lucas gestured towards his house. "We'll need our strength. Let's get some rest, and we'll tackle this head-on at dawn."

Together, they retraced their steps back inside, the letter a silent promise of trials yet to come. The calm before the storm had indeed been fleeting, and as they disappeared behind the closed door, the night seemed to hold its breath in anticipation of the gathering tempest.

Lucas's sneakers skidded across the dew-slick grass as he and Clara made their way to Willow Creek's central square at the break of dawn. The town was silent, save for the occasional chirp of waking birds. Their breaths hung in the cool air, mingling with the mist that clung to the cobblestones.

"Think anyone will show?" Clara asked, her voice low but carrying a clear note of hope.

"Edith said word spread fast after the last incident," Lucas replied. "If there are others like us, they'll be here."

They waited, the minutes stretching on, until the sound of approaching footsteps disrupted the calm. Two figures emerged from the mist: a girl with a shock of fiery red hair, and beside her, a tall boy with an earnest expression etched into his features.

"Hey, you're Lucas and Clara, right?" the girl called out, her voice strong and sure. "I'm Ruby, and this is my brother, Eli. We heard about what happened at the mansion. About Thomas."

Eli nodded, his gaze intense. "We've had our own... encounters. We want to help."

"Welcome aboard," Lucas said with a smile. "We could use more hands. The problem is bigger than we thought."

The group huddled together as Lucas unfolded the letter once again. Clara pointed to the cryptic symbols scrawled at the bottom. "These aren't just random. They're part of something ancient—something Edith couldn't fully translate."

"Let me see that," Ruby said, leaning in. Her eyes narrowed as she traced the symbols with a slender finger. "I've seen these before, in my granddad's old journals. He was into all this occult stuff."

"Can you make anything out?" Clara asked, hopeful.

"Maybe," Ruby replied. "But it'll take some time."

"Time we might not have," Eli added gravely. "There's something else we need to tell you."

The siblings exchanged a glance, and Ruby continued, "Last night, we saw something by the old mill. A shadow, but not like any regular shadow. It moved against the light, and it felt... wrong."

"Evil," Eli interjected.

"Like it wanted to consume everything in its path," Ruby finished.

"Could this be related to the letter?" Clara wondered aloud.

"Sounds like it could be our malevolent entity," Lucas said, his jaw tightening.

"Entity?" Ruby asked, curiosity piquing.

"According to the letter, there's something dangerous brewing. More than just a haunting," Clara explained. "It's targeting the town itself."

"Then we need to act, and quickly," Eli said decisively. "Whatever it is, it's gaining strength."

"First, we decipher this," Lucas said, waving the letter. "Ruby, you and your granddad's journals might be our best shot. Can you do it?"

"Absolutely," she confirmed with a determined nod.

"Good," Lucas said. "We stick together on this. Share everything we find. If there's something out there threatening Willow Creek, we'll face it as one."

"Agreed," the others chorused, their newfound alliance solidifying in the dim morning light.

"Let's meet back here after sunset," suggested Clara. "By then, we might have more answers."

"Or more questions," Lucas added under his breath, his green eyes reflecting the dawn's early rays, now tempered with the gravity of their task.

As the four parted ways, each to their own research and preparations, the town square seemed less desolate, the weight of the impending darkness a shared burden among new allies, united in purpose and resolve.

The setting sun cast a blood-orange glow over Willow Creek, igniting the windows of Edith Moore's library with an eerie semblance of fire. Inside, Lucas and Clara huddled around a weathered oak table that groaned under the weight of ancient texts, maps, and handwritten notes. They were not alone; their new allies—Ruby, Eli, and several others who had felt the tremors of darkness threatening their town—stood shoulder to shoulder with them.

"Salt, iron, sage... Is there anything we're missing?" Clara asked, her voice steady despite the gravity of their task.

"Courage," replied Lucas wryly, though his eyes never left the cryptic symbols scrawled across the parchment before him.

"Got plenty of that," Eli said, clapping Lucas on the back. "What we need is a plan."

"Right." Lucas straightened, a determined glint in his green eyes. "We know it draws power from the ley lines converging beneath the town square. If we can disrupt the flow..."

"Then we cut off its strength at the source," Ruby finished, tapping a spot on the map. "But it won't go quietly."

"Nothing ever does in this town," Clara murmured, but her gaze was fierce.

"Everyone knows what they're doing?" Lucas scanned the group, meeting each pair of eyes in turn. Nods rippled through the ranks like a silent wave of resolve.

"Then let's end this," he declared, shouldering his backpack filled with the gathered implements of their ritualistic arsenal.

Stepping out into the twilight, the air crackled with a charged expectancy. As they made their way towards the heart of Willow Creek, shadows danced ominously along the walls, whispering secrets only half-heard by the living.

"Stay sharp," Lucas warned as they approached the town square, where a dense fog had begun to coil around the base of the old water fountain, slithering across the cobblestones like a living thing.

"Here it comes," Clara said, her voice barely audible above the suddenly rising wind.

From the mist emerged a formless entity, a maelstrom of swirling darkness that chilled the soul. The malevolent force loomed before them, its presence oppressive, as if it sought to crush their spirits before even a blow was struck.

"Circle up!" Lucas commanded, and they hastily formed a ring around the fountain, each member clutching their chosen talisman.

"Recite the incantations exactly as Edith taught us," he instructed, his voice unwavering as he began to chant, the ancient words resonating with power.

"Animae antiqua, audite nos," Clara intoned alongside him, her voice growing stronger with each syllable.

"Revertar ad tenebras," the group chanted in unison, the sound gaining momentum.

The entity roared, a cacophony of despair and rage that threatened to drown out their voices, but they held firm. The ground trembled beneath their feet, cracks spider-webbing across the stone as if the earth itself was rebelling against the darkness.

"Keep going!" Lucas shouted, his mop of brown hair whipped wildly by the gale that now surrounded them.

"Protege domum nostram," they continued, clasping hands, their collective will embodied in a shimmering barrier that rose to meet the onslaught.

"Lucas, now!" Clara cried, her eyes locked onto the eye of the storm where the entity thrashed against their defenses.

With a deep breath, Lucas drew from his backpack a crystal vial, its contents glowing with a pure, radiant light. He uncorked it and hurled the liquid into the heart of the tempest.

A blinding flash enveloped the square, and for a moment, time stood still. Then, as quickly as it had come, the darkness dissipated, leaving behind only the gentle whisper of the wind and the soft patter of water from the fountain, now flowing once more.

As the last echoes of their battle faded into the night, silence fell upon Willow Creek. The group, panting and disheveled, slowly released their grip on one another, their gazes meeting in quiet triumph.

"We did it," Lucas breathed, allowing himself a small smile of relief. "We actually did it."

"Thanks to you," Clara said, her warm brown eyes reflecting pride and gratitude.

"Thanks to all of us," he corrected, looking around at the faces of their allies. "We're stronger together."

"Let's just hope it stays quiet for a while," Ruby said, but even as she spoke, they all knew that in a town like Willow Creek, peace was often just the calm before the next storm.

Lucas stood among the remnants of what had been their most perilous confrontation yet. The once-menacing sky was now painted with streaks of pink and orange as dawn began to break over Willow Creek. He could hear the townsfolk emerging from their homes, tentative but eager to embrace the newfound peace that had settled upon their quiet town.

"Lucas?" Clara's voice was a soft whisper against the morning breeze. "It's over, isn't it?"

He turned to her, his green eyes meeting hers. "Yes," he confirmed, the weight of their victory—and its cost—pressing heavily on his chest.

"Look, they're all coming out," she said, gesturing towards the townspeople who were now flooding into the streets, expressions of disbelief giving way to joyous relief.

"Clara, we should have done something more..." Lucas's voice faltered as he caught sight of a motionless figure lying a few feet away from where they stood.

Together, they walked towards the body, the silence around them deepening with each step. It was Ruby, one of their bravest allies, who had stood by them through the darkest hours of the night. Her sacrifice had given them the crucial moment they needed to defeat the entity.

Lucas knelt beside her, a tear escaping down his cheek. "Ruby, you didn't deserve this," he whispered, his heart heavy with a mix of sorrow and gratitude.

"Lucas, she knew the risks," Clara said gently, placing a trembling hand on his shoulder. "She fought with all her heart."

"I know, but why her? Why did it have to be her?" His voice was small in the vastness of their loss.

"Because that's what heroes do," Clara replied, her voice steady despite the tears streaming down her face. "They make the hard choices for the ones they love."

"Willow Creek will never forget what she did for us," Lucas said, gazing at the gathering crowd, their faces alight with the first rays of hope in what felt like an eternity.

"Neither will we," Clara added, her words a solemn vow. "We'll remember her bravery forever."

They stood there, two friends united in grief and triumph, as the sun rose higher, casting long shadows behind them. The battle was over, and Willow Creek was safe once again, but the victory was bittersweet.

In their hearts, they knew that with every challenge overcome, the memories of those lost would be the torches guiding them forward, illuminating the path of the guardians of Willow Creek.

Lucas knelt by the creek, the cool water flowing over his hands, washing away the grime and sweat from the long night. Behind him, Willow Creek stirred to life, its residents emerging like cautious deer into the dawn of a new day.

"Feels different, doesn't it?" Clara's voice was soft but sure as she settled beside him, her gaze reflecting the gentle current.

He nodded, letting the water slip through his fingers. "Like waking up from a nightmare you thought would never end."

"Except this time we did wake up," she said, watching a leaf twirl in an eddy before drifting downstream.

"Thanks to Ruby," Lucas murmured, the name invoking a silent tribute.

Clara placed a pebble into the creek, watching the ripples expand. "She'd want us to keep going, you know?"

"Keep going?" Lucas echoed, his eyes meeting hers.

"Protecting the town." Clara's words hung between them, not as a question, but as the unspoken truth of their bond.

"Like guardians?" he asked, the title feeling both strange and fitting on his tongue.

"Exactly." Clara's smile held a newfound determination. "We've seen too much to pretend everything's normal. We can't just forget."

"Then we won't." Lucas stood up, feeling the weight of responsibility settle onto his young shoulders. "We'll be ready for whatever comes next."

They walked back toward the town, the damaged buildings and broken windows a testament to the battle fought and won. People waved at them, their expressions weary but grateful. Whispers of 'heroes' followed them, but Lucas knew they were simply friends who refused to give up on each other, or their town.

"Lucas, Clara!" Edith Moore called out from across the street, her silver hair catching the sunlight. "The town council wants to organize a watch, make sure nothing like this happens again. They could use your insights."

"Count us in," Lucas replied without hesitation.

"Good," Edith said with a nod. "And there's something else... I've been doing some reading—"

"Of course you have," Clara interjected with a small laugh.

"—and I think there might be more to this town than even we realize. Old legends, unsolved mysteries..."

"More adventures?" Lucas felt the spark of curiosity ignite once again.

"Perhaps," Edith said, her eyes twinkling with the promise of untold stories.

"Then we'll face them together," Clara declared, reaching out to squeeze Lucas's hand.

"Like always," Lucas affirmed, his green eyes bright with the prospect of the unknown.

As they walked on, the town of Willow Creek began its slow recovery, the hum of community spirit weaving through the air like a healing spell. The scars would remain, but so would the memories of courage, friendship, and sacrifice. And for Lucas and Clara, the journey had only just begun.

The moon hung high, a silent sentinel over the town of Willow Creek, as Lucas and Clara made their way through the mist-laden cemetery with their group in tow. The beams of their flashlights danced off ancient tombstones, casting long shadows that seemed to play tricks on the eyes.

"Remember," Lucas whispered, his voice barely rising above the chorus of crickets, "we're not just here to explore; we're here to protect."

"Got it, boss," quipped Jenna, one of the newer recruits who had been drawn into their fold, her tone a mix of nerves and excitement.

Clara's soft giggle floated through the air, a gentle reminder of her presence. "Lucas isn't the boss, Jenna. We're a team here."

"Team Everhart-Milton," another member added, followed by a round of quiet laughter among the group.

Lucas let the camaraderie wash over him, grateful for each person who had chosen to stand beside them. They all shared the same fire, the same resolve that had been sparked by the events at the old mansion—a legacy left by their dear friend Thomas. His spirit might have been freed, but his influence remained, driving them forward.

"Here," Clara said, stopping by a particularly weathered gravestone. "This is where the sightings have been."

Lucas knelt, running his fingers over the etched name. "Evelyn Chambers," he read aloud. "We're here to help you find peace."

"Is that...?" Jenna pointed towards the woods where a faint glow hovered between the trees.

"Stay sharp," Lucas instructed, leading the group towards the light. Adrenaline surged through his veins, the familiar thrill of a new mystery unfolding before them.

As they approached, the glow intensified, shaping into the figure of a woman. Lucas could feel Clara's hand tighten around his own—a silent message of unity.

"Lucas, look!" Clara's voice trembled with discovery. "The pendant around her neck—it's part of the town's lore!"

"Then let's solve this together," Lucas responded. He stepped forward, addressing the spectral figure. "Evelyn, we want to understand your story."

The ghostly woman seemed to acknowledge them, her ethereal form pulsing with an otherworldly light. It was moments like these that solidified their purpose, that reminded them why they had banded together.

"Can you believe this all started because I couldn't resist poking around that old house?" Lucas mused, his eyes never leaving Evelyn's apparition.

Clara squeezed his hand again, whispering back, "And because Thomas needed us. He brought us all together."

"His bravery lives on through us," Lucas agreed, feeling the weight and warmth of their shared history. "Through every life we touch, every mystery we unravel."

"Every ghost we help find their way home," Clara added, her voice steady and sure.

"Exactly," Lucas affirmed, his eyes meeting hers, reflecting a bond that had only grown stronger through their trials.

Together, they turned their attention back to Evelyn, ready to guide another lost soul and keep the promise they had made—not just to their friend, but to the entire town of Willow Creek. The legacy of their fallen friend was more than memory; it was action, hope, and an ever-expanding family of those brave enough to face the darkness with them.

Lucas crouched beside an ancient tombstone, tracing the faded lettering with a finger as the moon cast ghostly shadows over the graveyard. Clara stood beside him, her breath misting in the cool night air. They were waiting, but Lucas felt a sense of calm that was new to him.

"Remember when we first started this?" Lucas asked, his voice low. "I was just a kid chasing after stories and hungry for adventure."

Clara chuckled softly. "You're still that kid, Lucas. You've just... grown. We both have."

He nodded, remembering the countless days spent poring over old books and legends, the nights filled with whispered conversations and plans. Each challenge they'd faced had been like a chisel, shaping him, teaching him about the strength found in unity and the power of unwavering determination.

"Thomas showed me what real courage looked like," Lucas continued, his eyes on the stars. "Facing the dark without flinching, even when you're scared. Especially when you're scared."

"Courage isn't the absence of fear, it's facing it head-on," Clara said, echoing words they had both come to live by. "And perseverance... sticking to the path even when it's strewn with obstacles."

"Like tonight might be," Lucas mused, standing up and brushing dirt from his jeans. The wind picked up, stirring the leaves around them, whispering secrets only the dead knew.

"Whatever happens, we'll deal with it. Together." Clara squared her shoulders, her gaze determined.

"Exactly. Together." Lucas smiled at her, feeling a surge of gratitude for the bond they shared. It was more than friendship; it was a kinship forged in the fires of shared trials and triumphs.

"Any sign of our elusive ghost?" Clara asked, shifting the topic back to the task at hand.

"Not yet, but if there's one thing I've learned, it's patience." Lucas glanced at the EMF reader in his hand, its lights steady and unblinking—for now.

A hush fell over the graveyard, and the air grew colder. Lucas felt it then, the subtle shift in the atmosphere, the prickling sensation on the back of his neck that heralded the approach of something otherworldly. He met Clara's eyes, and without a word, they both turned toward the mausoleum where they'd last encountered the restless spirit.

"Here we go," Lucas whispered, stepping forward with his heart pounding in his chest. Not from fear, but from the thrill of the unknown and the knowledge that he was no longer the same boy who had once dared to enter a cursed mansion.

"Ready when you are," Clara responded, her voice a beacon in the darkness.

Together, they moved into the shadow of the mausoleum, their equipment at the ready, prepared for whatever the night would unveil. Lucas knew that whatever came next, he was changed—stronger, wiser, and forever intertwined with the mysteries of Willow Creek and the souls that wandered within it.

WHISPERS IN THE GRAVEYARD

The wrought-iron gates of Oakridge Cemetery loomed before them, moonlight glinting off the rusted metal. Eddie Hurdle's breath plumed in the frigid air as he exchanged a nervous glance with Tomas Godwin. The graveyard beyond was a sea of shadowy tombstones, like jagged teeth jutting from the earth.

"You ready for this?" Eddie whispered, his voice barely audible over the wind rustling through bare tree branches.

Tomas nodded, his jaw set with determination. "As ready as I'll ever be."

Eddie's heart thundered in his chest as he pushed open the creaking gate. The sound echoed through the silent cemetery, making him wince. He took a tentative step forward, gravel crunching under his sneakers.

This is it, Eddie thought. *No turning back now.* His eyes darted from tombstone to tombstone, searching for any sign of movement in the shadows.

"Stay close," he murmured to Tomas as they ventured deeper into the graveyard.

Their footsteps seemed unnaturally loud as they picked their way between weathered headstones. Moonlight filtered through skeletal tree branches, casting eerie, dancing shadows across crumbling monuments. A chill ran down Eddie's spine that had nothing to do with the cold.

"Eddie," Tomas whispered urgently, grabbing his friend's arm. "Did you see that?"

Eddie's head whipped around, following Tomas's pointing finger. For a heart-stopping moment, he thought he glimpsed a flickering shape darting between two mausoleums. But then it was gone.

"Probably just our imaginations," Eddie said, trying to sound more confident than he felt. "Come on, let's keep moving."

As they wove through the cemetery, Eddie's mind raced. *What if we actually see a ghost? What then?* He'd spent countless hours reading about the paranormal, but being here, surrounded by centuries of buried dead, was entirely different.

"You think she's really here?" Tomas asked, his voice barely above a whisper.

Eddie swallowed hard. "Only one way to find out."

As if in answer to Tomas's question, a shimmering mist began to coalesce before them. Eddie's breath caught in his throat as the vapor took shape, solidifying into the ethereal form of a young girl. Her translucent figure flickered like candlelight in a breeze, her long hair seeming to float in an unseen current.

"Shannon," Eddie breathed, his voice a mix of awe and trepidation.

The spirit's sorrowful eyes locked onto the boys, drawing them closer with an inexplicable pull. Eddie felt his feet moving of their own accord, his fear giving way to fascination.

"You came," Shannon's voice whispered, an otherworldly echo that seemed to reverberate through Eddie's very bones. "I've waited so long."

Tomas gripped Eddie's arm tightly. "She's real," he hissed. "Eddie, she's actually real!"

Eddie nodded, unable to tear his gaze from Shannon's ghostly visage. Her face, though beautiful, was etched with a profound sadness that made his heart ache.

"What happened to you?" Eddie asked, his voice trembling slightly.

Shannon's form flickered, and for a moment, Eddie thought she might disappear. But then she spoke, her words carried on the night breeze.

"It was supposed to be a perfect day," she began, her ethereal voice tinged with longing. "Mom, Dad, and I were driving to the lake. We were laughing, singing along to the radio..."

Eddie felt a lump forming in his throat as Shannon's tale unfolded. He could almost see it - the happy family, the sunny day, the sudden screech of tires.

"The truck came out of nowhere," Shannon continued, her ghostly form shimmering with emotion. "There was a awful crash, and then... darkness."

Tomas let out a small gasp. "The accident on Route 7," he whispered. "I remember hearing about it."

Eddie's mind raced. He'd read about that crash in the local archives. Three lives lost in an instant - the Hurst family, wiped out in a single tragic moment.

"We never made it to the other side," Shannon's voice echoed mournfully through the cemetery. "My parents and I... we're lost. Separated. I've been searching for so long..."

Eddie felt a surge of compassion for the spectral girl before him. "We'll help you," he found himself saying. "We'll find a way to reunite you with your parents."

Shannon's form seemed to brighten slightly at his words, a flicker of hope in her ghostly eyes. "You would do that?" she asked, her voice a mixture of disbelief and gratitude.

As Eddie nodded, he realized the enormity of what he'd just promised. But looking at Shannon's sorrowful yet hopeful expression, he knew he couldn't turn back now.

Eddie's gaze met Tomas's, a silent understanding passing between them. Tomas's eyebrows furrowed with determination, a slight nod confirming his commitment. The moonlight cast long shadows across their faces, highlighting the resolve etched into their features.

"We're in this together," Tomas said, his voice barely above a whisper but filled with conviction.

Eddie felt a chill run down his spine, not from fear, but from the weight of their promise. "Shannon," he began, his voice cracking slightly, "we'll do whatever it takes to help you find peace."

The ghostly figure of Shannon flickered, her ethereal form seeming to pulse with a mix of hope and sorrow. "Thank you," she breathed, her words carried on a gust of wind that rustled the nearby trees.

As dawn broke the next day, Eddie and Tomas found themselves in the musty confines of the town archives. Dust motes danced in the shafts of sunlight streaming through grimy windows, settling on towering shelves packed with yellowed papers and leather-bound tomes.

"Where do we even start?" Tomas mumbled, running a hand through his tousled hair.

Eddie's fingers traced the spines of old newspapers, leaving inky smudges on his skin. "We need to find out everything we can about the Hurst family," he said, pulling out a heavy volume. "Their lives, the accident, where they're buried..."

As they delved deeper into the records, time seemed to blur. Pages rustled, microfiche whirred, and the boys' determination grew with each passing hour. Eddie's mind raced with possibilities, piecing together fragments of information like a complex puzzle.

"Tomas, look at this," Eddie called out, his voice tinged with excitement. He pointed to a faded newspaper clipping, its headline proclaiming a tragic accident on Route 7.

Tomas leaned in, his breath stirring up a small cloud of dust. "This could be the key," he said, eyes scanning the article. "But where does it lead us?"

Eddie's brow furrowed in concentration. "I'm not sure yet," he admitted, "but it's a start. We promised Shannon we'd help, and I intend to keep that promise."

As they continued their search, the weight of their task settled over them like a heavy cloak. Yet beneath the uncertainty, a spark of hope burned bright, fueling their resolve to unravel the mystery that bound Shannon's spirit to this world.

A soft clearing of the throat interrupted their intense focus. Eddie looked up, blinking as his eyes adjusted from the dim microfiche reader to the figure standing before them.

"You boys seem to be on quite the historical quest," a woman remarked, her voice gentle yet resonant with an undercurrent of curiosity.

Eddie straightened, taking in the newcomer's silver-streaked hair and kind eyes behind wire-rimmed glasses. "We're, uh, doing research for a school project," he stammered, exchanging a quick glance with Tomas.

The woman's lips curved into a knowing smile. "I'm Margaret Sinclair, the local historian," she introduced herself, extending a hand. "And I suspect your 'project' might benefit from a guide through our labyrinthine archives."

As Eddie shook her hand, he felt a surge of relief. Here was someone who might actually help them make sense of the scattered pieces they'd gathered. "I'm Eddie, and this is Tomas," he said. "We're looking into the Hurst family, actually. There was an accident..."

Margaret's eyes lit up with recognition. "Ah, the Hurst tragedy. A somber chapter in Oakridge's history, to be sure." She pulled up a chair, her movements deliberate and graceful. "What would you like to know?"

Eddie leaned forward, his heart racing. "Everything," he breathed. "Especially about their daughter, Shannon."

As Margaret began to speak, her words painted vivid pictures of Oakridge's past. Eddie found himself transported, seeing the town through the lens of decades gone by. Yet even as Margaret's wealth of knowledge opened new avenues of inquiry, a gnawing frustration began to build in Eddie's chest.

Hours passed, and still, the crucial piece they needed – the location of Shannon's parents' final resting place – eluded them. Eddie's fingers drummed restlessly on the table, leaving faint inky marks.

"There has to be something we're missing," he muttered, more to himself than to Tomas or Margaret. The weight of their promise to Shannon pressed down on him, a constant reminder of what was at stake.

Tomas shared his friend's frustration, rubbing his tired eyes. "Maybe we should call it a day, start fresh tomorrow?"

Eddie shook his head vehemently. "No, we can't give up. Shannon's counting on us." He turned to Margaret, desperation creeping into his voice. "Is there anything else? Any other records we haven't checked?"

Margaret's brow furrowed in thought. "Well, there are some older parish records that haven't been digitized yet. They're quite fragile, but..." She trailed off, studying Eddie's determined expression. "I suppose we could take a look, if you're willing to handle them with care."

Eddie nodded eagerly, a spark of hope reigniting. As Margaret led them deeper into the archives, he silently renewed his vow. No matter how long it took, they would find the answers Shannon needed. The chill of the cemetery night still lingered in his memory, driving him forward into the musty labyrinth of Oakridge's past.

The antique clock in Edgar Winters' parlor chimed nine, its sonorous tone reverberating through the dimly lit room. Eddie's eyes darted nervously around, taking in the bizarre collection of artifacts that adorned every surface. Crystal balls, weathered grimoires, and what looked unsettlingly like human bones vied for space on crowded shelves.

Tomas leaned in close, whispering, "Are you sure about this, Eddie? This place gives me the creeps."

Before Eddie could respond, a silky voice cut through the silence. "Doubts are natural when facing the unknown, young Tomas. But they can also blind us to the truth that lies just beyond our perception."

Edgar Winters materialized from the shadows, his silver-streaked hair catching the flickering candlelight. His piercing blue eyes seemed to look right through them, making Eddie's skin prickle.

"Mr. Winters," Eddie began, swallowing hard. "We need your help. There's a spirit—"

Edgar raised a hand, silencing him. "The young Hurst girl. Yes, I know. Her presence has been... unsettling the veil between worlds."

Eddie's heart raced. How could he possibly know about Shannon? He exchanged a bewildered glance with Tomas.

"You seek to aid her," Edgar continued, his voice a melodious whisper. "A noble endeavor, but one fraught with danger. The spirit realm is not to be trifled with lightly."

Tomas stepped forward, his voice steady despite his obvious unease. "We understand the risks, sir. But we made a promise."

A ghost of a smile played on Edgar's lips. "Promises to the dead carry great weight. Very well, I will guide you. But heed my words carefully, for they may be all that stands between you and the abyss."

Eddie felt a mix of relief and trepidation wash over him. As Edgar began to speak of ancient rituals and ethereal bridges, he couldn't shake the feeling that they were stepping into something far beyond their understanding. Yet the memory of Shannon's sorrowful face steeled his resolve. Whatever challenges lay ahead, they would face them together.

The musty scent of old leather and parchment filled Eddie's nostrils as he hunched over the ancient tome in the town archives. His fingers trembled as he traced the faded ink on the yellowed page, heart pounding in his chest. Beside him, Tomas leaned in close, his breath catching audibly.

"Eddie," Tomas whispered, voice tight with disbelief. "Look at this."

Eddie's eyes followed Tomas's pointing finger to a weathered map of Oakridge Cemetery. There, in a far corner, lay a plot marked "Unconsecrated Ground." His stomach lurched as he read the names scrawled beside it: "Hurst, Michael and Sarah."

"Shannon's parents," Eddie breathed, a chill running down his spine. "They're not in hallowed ground."

Tomas's face paled. "What does that mean for their souls?"

Eddie swallowed hard, remembering Edgar's cryptic warnings. "It means they're trapped, Tomas. Wandering. We have to help them."

The weight of their discovery pressed down on them like a physical force. Eddie's mind raced, piecing together the implications. "This is why Shannon can't move on. Her parents are stuck here too."

Tomas nodded grimly. "We need to go back to the cemetery. Tonight."

As the clock struck midnight, Eddie and Tomas stood at the gates of Oakridge Cemetery, their breath misting in the cold night air. The moon hung low and heavy, casting long shadows across the gravestones.

"Are you sure about this?" Tomas whispered, his usual bravado faltering.

Eddie clenched his fists, steeling himself. "We made a promise, remember? Shannon's counting on us."

They stepped into the graveyard, gravel crunching beneath their feet. The air seemed to thicken around them, pressing in from all sides. Eddie's heart hammered in his chest, every snapping twig and rustling leaf setting his nerves on edge.

"I can't shake the feeling we're being watched," Tomas murmured, eyes darting nervously.

Eddie nodded, his own skin prickling with unseen eyes. "Stay close. We need to find that unconsecrated ground."

As they ventured deeper into the cemetery, the shadows seemed to writhe and twist, taking on lives of their own. Eddie clutched the amulet Edgar had given him, its weight reassuring against his chest. Whatever forces they were about to confront, they weren't going in unprepared.

"There," Tomas hissed, pointing to a dark corner of the graveyard. "That must be it."

Eddie's breath caught in his throat as they approached. The air here felt different – heavier, charged with an energy that made his hair stand on end. He could almost hear whispers on the wind, fleeting and just beyond comprehension.

"We're here to help," he called out, voice shaking despite his best efforts. "Shannon, if you can hear us, we're here to reunite you with your parents."

The wind picked up, swirling around them with unnatural force. Eddie's heart pounded, a mix of fear and determination coursing through him. Whatever came next, they were ready to face it – for Shannon, for her parents, and for the promise they'd made.

The wind howled, carrying with it a cacophony of whispers that seemed to come from everywhere and nowhere at once. Eddie squinted against the sudden gust, his eyes widening as ghostly figures began to materialize around them.

"Eddie," Tomas gasped, grabbing his friend's arm. "Look!"

Spectral forms, translucent and shimmering, emerged from the shadows. Some wore clothing from decades past, while others appeared in more modern attire. Their faces were a mix of confusion, sorrow, and longing.

Eddie's throat tightened. "Lost souls," he whispered. "They're all trapped here."

As the apparitions pressed closer, Eddie felt a chill run through his body. He steeled himself, remembering Shannon's sorrowful eyes and the promise they'd made.

"We're not here for you," he called out, his voice stronger than he felt. "But we're trying to help someone find peace. Please, let us pass."

The spirits hesitated, their whispers growing louder. Eddie could almost make out words now – pleas for help, cries of anguish, and fragments of forgotten memories.

Tomas stepped forward, his face pale but determined. "We're looking for Shannon Hurst's parents. Does anyone know where they are?"

A ripple seemed to pass through the crowd of spirits. Slowly, they began to part, forming a path through the unconsecrated ground.

"I think they're showing us the way," Eddie murmured, his heart racing. "Come on."

As they walked, Eddie couldn't shake the feeling of countless eyes upon them. He tried to focus on their goal, on Shannon's ethereal face and the peace they hoped to bring her.

Suddenly, a familiar figure appeared before them, her form flickering like candlelight in the darkness.

"Shannon," Eddie breathed, relief washing over him.

The ghostly girl's eyes were wide with a mix of hope and fear. "You came," she whispered, her voice echoing strangely in the night air. "But it's dangerous here. The others... they're restless."

"We're not leaving without helping you," Tomas said firmly. "Where are your parents?"

Shannon's form wavered, and for a moment Eddie feared she might disappear entirely. But then she steadied, pointing towards two weathered gravestones nearby.

"There," she said, her voice barely audible. "But I can't reach them. Something's keeping us apart."

Eddie exchanged a determined look with Tomas. Whatever force was at work here, they were prepared to face it. For Shannon, and for all the lost souls trapped in this lonely place.

The first hints of dawn painted the sky in muted hues of pink and gold as Eddie and Tomas stumbled out of the cemetery gates. Their clothes were disheveled, smudged with dirt and dew, and their eyes held a haunted look that spoke of things unseen by mortal eyes. The graveyard behind them lay silent once more, its secrets buried deep beneath the earth.

Eddie's legs felt like lead as he collapsed onto the damp grass just beyond the cemetery's iron fence. He sucked in a deep breath, the crisp morning air filling his lungs and grounding him in reality once more.

"We did it," he whispered, his voice hoarse. "We actually did it."

Tomas slumped down beside him, running a trembling hand through his tousled hair. "Yeah," he breathed, "but at what cost? I feel like... like I've aged a hundred years in one night."

Eddie turned to look at his friend, noting the new lines of tension around Tomas's eyes. "I know what you mean. But we helped her, Tom. We helped Shannon and her parents find peace."

A comfortable silence fell between them as they watched the sun slowly climb above the horizon, its warm rays chasing away the last vestiges of the night's terrors.

"Do you think..." Tomas began, hesitating. "Do you think we'll ever be the same after this?"

Eddie considered the question, feeling the weight of their shared experience settle deep in his bones. "No," he said finally. "But maybe that's not such a bad thing. We've seen beyond the veil, Tom. We know there's more to this world than meets the eye."

Tomas nodded slowly, a wry smile tugging at his lips. "We're ghost whisperers now, huh? Regular supernatural detectives."

Eddie chuckled, the sound dispelling some of the lingering tension. "I guess so. Partners in the paranormal."

As they sat there, watching the world awaken around them, Eddie felt a profound sense of change settling over him. The bond between him and Tomas had been forged anew in the crucible of their otherworldly adventure. They had faced the unknown together and emerged victorious, forever altered but unbroken.

"Whatever comes next," Eddie said softly, "we face it together. Deal?"

Tomas reached out, clasping Eddie's hand in a firm grip. "Deal."

And as the sun climbed higher, bathing them in its golden light, Eddie knew that while the night had changed them irrevocably, it had also given them something precious: an unshakeable friendship and the knowledge that they could overcome even the most impossible of odds.

GHOSTS OF WESTWARD HIGH

The musty scent of aged paper enveloped Joyce as her slender fingers traced the yellowed margins of the biology textbook. Her eyes, magnified behind thick-rimmed glasses, narrowed as they caught an anomaly—faded ink etched into the page's edge. Heart quickening, she leaned closer, her ponytail brushing against the weathered spine.

"What secrets do you hold?" she whispered, deciphering the cryptic message: "Beware the eclipse. They will return."

A chill ran down Joyce's spine, but her analytical mind whirred into action. This was no mere graffiti; it held purpose, a clue to something greater. She had to know more.

Clutching the book to her chest, Joyce weaved through the labyrinth of shelves, her footsteps echoing in the hushed library. She spotted Brian and Kyle in their usual corner, bathed in the warm glow of a reading lamp.

"Guys, you won't believe what I found," Joyce breathed, sliding into the chair beside them.

Brian looked up from his phone, eyebrow arched. "Let me guess, another riveting chapter on mitochondria?"

Joyce ignored his sarcasm, spreading the book open. "Look at this message. It's not just random scribbling."

Kyle leaned in, his artist's eyes scrutinizing the faded ink. "It does seem... deliberate," he murmured, a hint of intrigue in his soft voice.

"Oh come on," Brian scoffed, rolling his eyes. "It's probably some bored kid from the '80s trying to freak people out. You're not seriously buying into this, are you?"

Joyce felt a flare of irritation. "It's more than that, Brian. This could be connected to the school's history, maybe even explain some of the strange occurrences people have reported."

Kyle nodded slowly, his fingers twitching as if itching to sketch the mysterious message. "There have been rumors about this place for years," he said, his voice barely above a whisper.

Brian leaned back, crossing his arms. "Rumors, exactly. Ghost stories to scare freshmen. You two are too smart to fall for this nonsense."

Joyce's mind raced, piecing together fragments of local lore and historical tidbits. "But what if it's not nonsense? What if there's truth behind the legends?"

Kyle's eyes widened. "You want to investigate, don't you?"

Joyce nodded, determination etched across her features. "We have to. This could be the key to understanding what's really going on at Westward High."

Brian groaned. "And here I thought we'd have a normal senior year. Fine, I'll play along, but only to prove there's nothing supernatural going on."

As Joyce launched into her plan, her voice hushed but intense, she couldn't shake the feeling that they were standing on the precipice of something monumental. The library's shadows seemed to deepen around them, as if the very walls were listening, holding their breath in anticipation of what was to come.

The fluorescent lights flickered ominously as Joyce, Brian, and Kyle crept through the deserted hallways of Westward High. Their footsteps echoed in the empty corridor, each sound amplified in the eerie silence. Joyce's heart raced, her mind cataloging every detail of their surroundings.

"This is ridiculous," Brian muttered, his voice tight with unease despite his skepticism. "We shouldn't be here after hours."

Joyce shushed him, her eyes darting to the shadows that seemed to dance at the edge of her vision. "Keep your voice down. We need to find that archive room."

As they rounded a corner, the lights above them sputtered and dimmed, casting long, distorted shadows on the walls. Kyle stumbled, grabbing Joyce's arm. "Did you see that?" he whispered, pointing to a flickering bulb.

Joyce's brow furrowed. "It's just faulty wiring," she said, more to convince herself than her friends. But a chill ran down her spine as the light seemed to follow their movements, brightening and dimming in their wake.

"Over here," Brian called softly, gesturing to a door with peeling paint. "This looks promising."

Joyce approached, her hand trembling slightly as she turned the handle. The door creaked open, revealing a musty room filled with shelves of old books and boxes.

"Jackpot," she breathed, her academic curiosity overtaking her fear. She moved purposefully to a stack of yearbooks, her fingers tracing their spines.

"1960s... perfect," Joyce murmured, pulling out a dusty volume. As she opened it, a newspaper clipping fluttered to the floor. Kyle bent to retrieve it, his eyes widening as he scanned the headline.

"Guys, look at this," he said, voice quavering. "'Westward High Rocked by Tragic Hazing Incident.'"

Joyce snatched the article, her analytical mind already piecing together connections. "This must be what the message was referring to," she said, excitement and dread mingling in her voice.

As they huddled around the clipping, the room seemed to grow colder. Joyce couldn't shake the feeling that they were being watched, that the very walls of Westward High were closing in around them, guarding long-buried secrets that were finally coming to light.

The air in the archive room grew thick with dust and tension as Joyce pored over the newspaper clipping. Suddenly, a faint whisper echoed through the corridors, sending a shiver down her spine.

"Did you hear that?" Joyce asked, her voice barely above a whisper.

Kyle nodded, his eyes wide with apprehension. "It sounded like... like someone saying 'unfinished business.'"

Brian scoffed, but Joyce noticed his confident demeanor falter slightly. "Come on, guys. It's probably just the wind or some stupid prank."

The whispers grew louder, seeming to bounce off the walls around them. Joyce's heart raced as she tried to make sense of the ethereal voices. "This isn't right," she thought, her analytical mind struggling to rationalize the inexplicable.

"We should go," Kyle suggested, his slender frame visibly trembling.

As they turned to leave, the lights flickered violently. Joyce felt a sudden chill envelop her, as if she'd been plunged into icy water. The room spun, and when it settled, she found herself alone in a dim, distorted version of the archive room.

A figure materialized before her, translucent and shimmering with an otherworldly glow. Joyce's breath caught in her throat as she recognized her own features in the apparition's face, twisted with disappointment and resentment.

"You'll never be good enough," the ghost hissed, its voice a cruel echo of Joyce's own. "All that work, all those sleepless nights, and for what? You're destined to fail."

Joyce stumbled backward, her glasses slipping down her nose. "No, that's not true," she stammered, but doubt crept into her voice.

The ghost pressed closer, its eyes boring into Joyce's soul. "You're nothing without your grades, your achievements. What happens when you can't measure up?"

Joyce's mind raced, memories of late-night study sessions and her parents' expectant faces flashing before her eyes. "I... I'm more than just my accomplishments," she said, but the words felt hollow.

The apparition laughed, a chilling sound that reverberated through Joyce's bones. "Prove it," it challenged, its form flickering like a faulty television screen.

Joyce closed her eyes, trying to center herself. "This isn't real," she thought desperately. "I am Joyce Buckner. I am capable. I am worthy." But as she opened her eyes, the ghost's resentful gaze bore into her, forcing her to confront the crushing weight of expectations she'd carried for so long.

Brian's heart pounded as he rounded the corner, desperate to escape the whispers that had followed Joyce. His breath came in ragged gasps, fogging up the dim hallway. Suddenly, the air around him turned icy, and a familiar voice echoed from the shadows.

"Brian Harris, always running away," the voice taunted, dripping with disdain. Brian spun around, his eyes widening as he saw a translucent figure materialize before him. The ghost bore an eerie resemblance to his childhood best friend, Jake.

"This isn't real," Brian muttered, his trademark skepticism wavering. "You're not Jake."

The apparition's laughter cut through him like shards of glass. "Oh, but I am. Remember how you abandoned me when I needed you most?"

Brian's stomach churned as memories flooded back - Jake's parents' divorce, the day he'd chosen popularity over friendship. "I-I didn't mean to," he stammered, his usual confidence crumbling.

"Didn't you?" the ghost sneered, circling Brian. "Just like you'll abandon Joyce and Kyle when things get tough."

"No!" Brian shouted, his voice echoing off the lockers. "I've changed. I'm loyal now."

The ghost's eyes glinted maliciously. "Are you? Or are you just waiting for the right moment to betray them too?"

Brian's mind raced, doubt seeping into his thoughts. He thought of Joyce's determined face, Kyle's quiet strength. "They're my friends," he insisted, but his voice trembled.

"For now," the ghost whispered, its form flickering. "But how long until you let them down?"

As Brian grappled with his inner turmoil, Kyle found himself alone in the art room, surrounded by easels casting long shadows in the moonlight. The hairs on the back of his neck stood up as he felt an unseen presence.

"Kyle," a soft voice called, seeming to come from everywhere and nowhere at once. "Why do you even bother?"

Kyle's breath hitched as a ghostly figure emerged from the shadows, its features an unsettling blend of all the people who had ever rejected him. "What do you mean?" he asked, his voice barely above a whisper.

The apparition glided closer, its eyes pools of emptiness. "Your art, your friendship, your very existence - it's all meaningless. No one truly understands you, do they?"

Kyle's hand trembled as he reached for a nearby pencil, an instinctive need to create, to express himself. "That's not true," he murmured, but doubt crept into his voice.

"Isn't it?" the ghost taunted. "Remember how your family dismissed your passion? How your classmates mocked your sketches?"

Tears welled in Kyle's eyes as painful memories resurfaced. "Joyce and Brian accept me," he said, his voice cracking.

The apparition's laughter was a cold wind through Kyle's soul. "For now. But soon, they'll see how worthless you really are."

Kyle's grip tightened on the pencil, his knuckles turning white. "I'm not worthless," he whispered, more to himself than the ghost.

"Prove it," the spirit hissed, its form rippling like a mirage. "Show them you're worthy of acceptance, of love."

As Kyle stood frozen, torn between his fears and his desperate need for belonging, the ghost's whispers continued to echo through the room, each word chipping away at his fragile sense of self-worth.

The fluorescent lights flickered ominously as Joyce burst into the empty classroom, her glasses askew and her usually neat ponytail coming undone. Brian stumbled in after her, his face ashen, followed closely by Kyle, whose eyes darted nervously around the room.

"Did you... did you see them too?" Joyce asked, her voice quavering as she gripped the edge of a desk for support.

Brian slumped into a chair, running his trembling hands through his hair. "I don't know what I saw," he muttered. "It couldn't have been real. Ghosts aren't real."

Kyle hugged himself, his fingers digging into his arms. "It felt real," he whispered. "Too real."

Joyce's analytical mind raced, searching for a logical explanation. But the chill that lingered in her bones and the haunting whispers echoing in her ears defied reason. She took a deep breath, trying to steady herself. "We need to approach this rationally. What exactly did each of us experience?"

As Brian recounted his encounter, his voice grew bitter. "It knew things, Joyce. Things I've never told anyone." His eyes narrowed suspiciously. "How could it know unless... unless one of you told it?"

"What? No!" Kyle exclaimed, his voice cracking. "Why would we do that?"

Joyce felt a pang of hurt at Brian's accusation. "Brian, we're your friends. We wouldn't betray you like that."

Brian scoffed, his skepticism morphing into paranoia. "Then how do you explain it? Maybe this is all some elaborate prank you two cooked up."

"It's not a prank!" Joyce snapped, her own fear and frustration bubbling to the surface. "I saw... I experienced... Look, we need to figure this out together."

Kyle nodded eagerly, desperate for unity. "Joyce is right. We can't turn on each other now."

As the tension in the room thickened, Joyce's eyes fell on an old bookshelf in the corner. Something about it nagged at her subconscious. She approached it slowly, her fingers tracing the dusty spines until they caught on a small, leather-bound journal wedged between two textbooks.

"What's that?" Brian asked, his curiosity momentarily overriding his suspicion.

Joyce carefully opened the journal, her eyes widening as she scanned its yellowed pages. "It's... it's a diary," she breathed. "From 1965."

Kyle peered over her shoulder. "What does it say?"

Joyce's voice trembled as she read aloud, "September 15th, 1965. The seniors are planning something big for initiation night. They say it'll be unforgettable. I'm scared, but I can't back out now. If I do, I'll never belong."

The trio exchanged uneasy glances as the weight of the words sank in. Joyce continued reading, her face growing paler with each sentence. The journal detailed a hazing ritual gone horribly wrong, resulting in multiple deaths that had been covered up by the school.

"Oh god," Brian whispered, his skepticism crumbling. "The ghosts... they're the victims of this hazing incident."

Kyle's eyes widened in horror. "They want justice," he realized. "That's why they're haunting the school."

Joyce closed the journal with shaking hands, her mind reeling from the revelation. "We've uncovered a decades-old crime," she said, her voice a mix of fear and determination. "And now the ghosts want us to set things right."

The classroom fell silent as the gravity of their situation sank in. The spirits that haunted Westward High were no longer just terrifying apparitions – they were the echoes of a tragic injustice, crying out for resolution. And somehow, Joyce, Brian, and Kyle had become entangled in their spectral quest for vengeance.

The classroom's silence was shattered by a sudden, ominous rumble. Joyce rushed to the window, her heart pounding. The moon hung low and heavy in the sky, its edge already darkening.

"The lunar eclipse," she breathed, her voice barely above a whisper. "It's starting."

Brian joined her, his face ashen. "What does that mean for us?"

Kyle, still clutching the journal, spoke up. "In paranormal lore, lunar eclipses are said to amplify spiritual energies. If that's true..."

"The ghosts will become stronger," Joyce finished, her analytical mind racing. "More corporeal. We don't have much time."

As if on cue, the lights flickered, and a bone-chilling whisper echoed through the room. "Justice... we seek justice..."

"We need to act now," Joyce declared, her determination overshadowing her fear. "There must be a way to confront them, to end this."

Brian, his earlier skepticism now replaced with grim acceptance, nodded. "But how? Where?"

Joyce's eyes lit up with realization. "The tunnels. The old maintenance tunnels beneath the school. That's where it happened, isn't it?"

Kyle flipped through the journal, nodding. "According to this, yes. That's where the hazing took place."

The trio exchanged nervous glances, the weight of their decision hanging heavy in the air. Joyce took a deep breath, steeling herself. "We have to go down there. It's our only chance to end this before the ghosts become too powerful."

With trembling hands, they gathered their flashlights and made their way to the school's basement. The door to the maintenance tunnels loomed before them, its rusty hinges groaning in protest as Brian pushed it open.

Joyce's flashlight beam cut through the darkness, revealing a narrow, damp corridor stretching endlessly before them. The air was thick with the musty scent of decay and something else... something otherworldly.

"Stay close," Joyce whispered, her voice echoing unnervingly in the confined space.

As they descended deeper into the bowels of the school, the walls seemed to close in around them. Their flashlights cast long, dancing shadows that played tricks on their eyes, making them jump at every flicker of movement.

The sound of their footsteps echoed off the damp walls, creating an eerie symphony that set their nerves on edge. Joyce couldn't shake the feeling that with each step, they were walking deeper into the ghosts' domain.

"Does anyone else feel like we're being watched?" Kyle whispered, his voice tight with fear.

Before anyone could answer, a cold breeze swept through the tunnel, extinguishing their flashlights and plunging them into total darkness.

The darkness pressed in like a living thing, suffocating and oppressive. Joyce's heart thundered in her chest as she fumbled with her flashlight, her usually steady hands shaking.

"Guys?" she called out, her voice cracking. "Are you there?"

"I'm here," Brian's voice came from her left, uncharacteristically tense. "Kyle?"

A whimper echoed through the tunnel, sending chills down Joyce's spine.

Suddenly, the air around them shifted, growing dense and charged with an otherworldly energy. Joyce's flashlight flickered back to life, revealing a scene straight out of her nightmares.

Before them stood three spectral figures, their forms flickering and twisting like smoke caught in a breeze. Each ghost seemed to lock onto one of the trio, their hollow eyes burning with an unnatural light.

The ghost facing Joyce took the form of a stern-looking woman, her features twisted into a disapproving scowl. "You'll never be good enough," it hissed, its voice a cacophony of whispers. "All your hard work, all your studying, and you'll still fail."

Joyce stumbled back, her mind reeling. "No," she whispered, her voice trembling. "That's not true."

To her right, she heard Brian's sharp intake of breath. His ghost, a shadowy figure with glowing red eyes, circled him menacingly. "They'll all leave you," it taunted. "Just like before. You can't trust anyone."

Kyle's ghost, a towering, faceless entity, loomed over him. "You don't belong," it intoned, its voice echoing with loneliness. "You never have, and you never will."

Joyce watched as Kyle crumpled to the ground, his hands covering his ears. Brian stood frozen, his eyes wide with disbelief and fear.

"We have to fight back," Joyce said, her voice stronger than she felt. "Remember why we're here. We're stronger together!"

As if in response to her words, the tunnel began to shake. Dust and small debris rained down on them as the lunar eclipse reached its peak, amplifying the ghosts' power.

The spectral figures lunged forward, their forms becoming more solid with each passing second. Joyce felt icy fingers brush against her skin, sending waves of despair through her body.

"The truth," she gasped, fighting against the overwhelming feeling of hopelessness. "We need to tell the truth about what happened!"

Brian's voice cut through the chaos, strong and clear. "It wasn't your fault!" he shouted. "The hazing, the accident - it was never meant to go that far!"

Kyle, still on the ground, looked up with tear-filled eyes. "You were victims too," he added softly. "Trapped by silence and guilt for all these years."

As they spoke, Joyce felt a shift in the air. The ghosts' forms began to waver, their expressions changing from malevolence to confusion.

"Keep going," Joyce urged her friends. "We're getting through to them!"

The oppressive chill in the air began to dissipate, like ice melting under the first warm rays of spring. Joyce's heart raced as she watched the ghosts' forms flicker and fade, their once-menacing presence now wavering like candlelight in a gentle breeze.

"Look," Brian whispered, his voice a mix of awe and relief. "They're... changing."

Joyce nodded, her analytical mind racing to make sense of the transformation. "It's working," she breathed. "Our acknowledgment of their pain, it's weakening their hold."

The spectral figures now hovered before them, their expressions no longer contorted with rage but softened with a sorrowful acceptance. One ghost, a young man with hollow eyes, drifted closer.

"We've carried this burden for so long," he said, his voice a haunting echo. "The truth... it's all we ever wanted."

Kyle, finding his courage, stepped forward. "And we'll make sure it's told," he promised, his voice trembling but sincere. "Your story won't be forgotten."

Joyce felt a surge of hope, but caution tempered her optimism. "Is this enough?" she asked, addressing the spirits directly. "Will you be able to rest now?"

The ghosts exchanged glances, their forms shimmering with uncertainty. The young man spoke again, his words tinged with both hope and hesitation.

"We feel the curse weakening, but..."

"But what?" Brian interjected, tension evident in his voice.

"The eclipse is ending," Joyce realized aloud, noticing the changing quality of the shadows around them. "And with it, their power to communicate."

The spirits began to fade, their voices becoming fainter. "There's more," one whispered. "Deeper secrets... buried in the school's past..."

As the last ethereal wisps dissipated, Joyce turned to her friends, her mind already formulating their next steps. "We've made progress, but this isn't over," she said firmly. "There's still work to be done."

Kyle nodded, a mix of determination and fear in his eyes. "Do you think we've really weakened the curse?"

Joyce bit her lip, uncertainty gnawing at her. "I hope so, but until we uncover those deeper secrets, I don't think we can be sure."

The tunnel fell silent, the oppressive atmosphere lifted but replaced by a lingering sense of unfinished business. As they made their way back towards the school proper, Joyce couldn't shake the feeling that they had only scratched the surface of Westward High's dark history.

About the Author

JT WULF is a best selling author in the genres of horror and suspense thriller. His books include: The Transition Hole, Dead, The Inn, The Cellar Door, The RIP Club, A Town Called Thereafter, Karma: The Final Payment

Read more at https://jaytwulf.com/.

About the Publisher

As a boutique book publisher, we take on only a few new authors per year. We focus on building an author's brand, thereby directing more resources towards their overall success. Authors accepted by True American Publishing become creative partners, therefore, participating in their own success.

Milton Keynes UK
Ingram Content Group UK Ltd.
UKHW031045291124
451807UK00001B/122